DEF CON ONE

John Simpson

Dreamspinner Press

Published by
Dreamspinner Press
4760 Preston Road
Suite 244-149
Frisco, TX 75034
http://www.dreamspinnerpress.com/

Def Con One

Cover Art by Dan Skinner/Cerberus Inc. cerberusinc@hotmail.com
Cover Design by Mara McKennen

ISBN: 978-1-935192-59-6

Printed in the United States of America
First Edition
February, 2009

eBook edition available
eBook ISBN: 978-1-935192-60-2

This book is dedicated to all the men and women who are gay and serving in the United States military while having to live under the policy of "Don't ask, Don't tell." We remember the service of all the gay veterans who have sacrificed much and have even given their lives while winning medals as high as the Congressional Medal of Honor. May all be allowed to serve openly in the near future and enjoy their lives more fully as a result.

CHAPTER 1

IT was a dangerous time in the world when I arrived at my first base assignment, fresh out of boot camp and security police training school. I ducked as a trash can flew over my head, signaling one of the fierce windstorms that swept this part of the country occasionally. The wind was so strong that trash cans were blowing through the air sideways. I hoped that wasn't a harbinger of things to come.

Tensions in the world were rising rapidly as a renewed Soviet Union rose from its own ashes at the conclusion of the first cold war. The Red Army was on the march once again in its attempt to reclaim a lost empire. American President David Windsor was warning the Soviet premier against expansion into the Balkans after it had reoccupied the former Soviet satellite country of Georgia. The risen Phoenix had talons and they were being used.

The Soviet response was to launch a brand new advanced Typhoon class nuclear submarine, the *Dmitrii Donskoy*, armed with the latest missile technology. This sub and its sister, the *Yuri Dolgorukii*, represented an increased threat to world peace and constituted a direct challenge to the West and in particular, the United States.

American satellite intelligence spotted the movement of mobile Soviet ICBM launchers throughout the Ural Mountains, indicating planning and strategy for possible future use in a hot war. These missiles were capable of conveying nuclear destruction to any part of the world.

Additional activity observed by satellite intelligence showed increased activity at Soviet *Spetsnaz* bases, or Russian Special Forces. To all outward appearances, it looked as if the Soviets were getting ready for a war that could include all or a portion of their various force capabilities.

This was my welcome to Francis E. Warren Air Force Base in Cheyenne, Wyoming, during the late summer of 2012. I was young at only 19, with very short blond hair courtesy of boot camp, blue eyes, 6′1″, and 180 pounds of muscle. I was an expert marksman with both the standard issue M16 and 9 mm Glock handgun. I had scored proficient with the shotgun and M60, belt-fed, air-cooled machine gun.

Warren Air Force Base was a "SAC" base during the early years of missiles; however, the Strategic Air Command had been done away with by the Air Force and the base now resided in the "90th Space Wing" of the Air Force Space Command. Warren was a particularly important Air Force base to the American defense capability as it controlled 120 intercontinental ballistic missiles, each armed with multiple warheads capable of destroying a large nation with one strike.

My orders required that I report to the First Sergeant's office upon arriving on base where I would be signed in, given orders, and assigned a barracks room. My first day or two would mostly be orientation of the base, my squadron, and the base police flight that I would be assigned to.

I was filled with nervous anticipation at what lay ahead. When I entered the Squadron clerical office, I observed at least seven airmen of different ranks involved in one task or another. I stopped an Airman First Class and told him I was reporting in for duty.

"Hey, Sergeant Davenport, over here, please. We have a new man coming on board!" the airman yelled.

"Thanks," I said to the airman.

A staff sergeant came over to me and took my orders. "Have a seat over there while I look at your paperwork," he said.

As I waited on the sergeant to finish, I began to fidget. I knew that I would have to formally report to the first sergeant and that was never a comfortable task for some reason. I suppose after being in an atmosphere of nothing but very low-echelon airmen, to report to a man who had seven stripes on his sleeves made me a bit uneasy.

"Okay, everything looks good. I'll see if the first sergeant can see you now."

My eyes followed the staff sergeant into another office. A man who must be the first sergeant took my file, glanced at it quickly and then said something to the staff sergeant, who came out of the office and told me to report to the man behind the desk.

I entered the office and stood at attention. "Airman Bryce Callahan reporting for duty as ordered, First Sergeant."

"Callahan, good to have you with us. Sit down while I look your file over," First Sergeant Peter Jordon said.

As I waited, I looked around the walls of the office at the many different citations and awards the first sergeant had acquired during his career. He was a senior master sergeant with only one grade left in the enlisted ranks of the Air Force unless he was made the first sergeant of the entire Air Force, which was a truly monumental task to accomplish. Sergeant Jordon looked to be in his late forties or early fifties, and was as fit as any airman in basic training.

"You graduated first in your Security Police training squadron, I see. Outstanding. We'll put your talents to good use here at Warren. Your duties may be split between base law enforcement and security in the missile fields. You should have your top secret security clearance in a matter of days if it's not already on base now. Tomorrow you will report to the Orderly room in the barracks for your briefings along with all the other new men arriving today. Uniform of the day will be combat fatigues and you will report precisely at 0800 hours. Any questions?"

"Yes, First Sergeant. Is there someone who can show me where the mess hall is so that I can eat dinner tonight and breakfast tomorrow morning?"

"When you report in to the barracks, the CQ, or man in charge of quarters, will have someone take you over to the chow hall. He can also show you the other main buildings that you'll need to know. My door is always open and that means if you have a problem, you talk to me or your flight commander. Understood?"

"Yes, First Sergeant."

"Sergeant Davenport will have you taken over to the barracks. Make sure you're on time in the morning. That's all."

Another young airman showed me to the barracks and introduced me to the sergeant on duty. It was his job to assign me to a room and get me anything else I needed for the immediate moment. I thanked the airman and started the process for signing in to the barracks.

"Here are two towels, washcloth, and soap. Everything else, you need to supply. In fact, if you want decent towels, you need to buy your own. I'm putting you in a room by yourself for now, but that won't last so don't get used to it. You're in room two-twenty. Chow is from five to seven- thirty and you'll need to present this meal card to get service. Briefings begin at 0800. Don't be late."

I took the towels and found my room. It was nothing fancy by any means. It held a bunk bed, two desks, two dressers, and two closets, and had one window. The floor was without carpeting and the room was painted white, like the rest of the barracks. It had the distinct smell of cleaning solutions and floor wax. I unpacked my duffel bag and tried to make the room seem less institutional by putting some personal things out on my desk and dresser. I took the bottom bunk; if I had to share the room one day, he could take the top.

As I didn't have very much to put away in the first place, it took no time to accomplish the task. The biggest issue was trying to get some of the wrinkles out of my uniforms that had been folded up in my duffel bag. It was just after 1600 hours – 4:00 – and I decided to take a short walk around the base. As I left the barracks I noted that the wind had died down to a reasonable level and I was no longer in danger of getting hit by a trash can or some other flying object. I headed over to the base theater to see what movies were in and coming soon. From there I walked past the Police Station for the base and noted cars coming and going. I was so caught up in seeing everything that I passed a second lieutenant without saluting. You would have thought the world had ended.

"Airman, didn't you see the bars on my shoulders?" the young lieutenant asked with an indignant glare.

I came to attention and saluted the officer. "I'm sorry, sir. I just arrived on base and I guess I got caught up in looking at everything."

"Very well. Don't let it happen again, airman. Carry on."

"Yes, sir," I replied as I gave a second salute and walked away.

Young lieutenants were very mindful that they were owed a salute by all enlisted men. I would come to learn in time that new lieutenants could be one of the greater pains in the ass to any enlisted man. I walked pass the NCO club that was strictly for non-commissioned officers and which I would not be allowed to enter until I had two more stripes added to the one I had now on my arms. This would take probably another two years to achieve.

I noticed that it was now time for dinner so I headed back to the dining hall to eat. The food was very good, as it had been in basic training and technical school. Comfort was one of the things that the

Air Force was known for and which certainly didn't detract from my decision to enlist. I ate by myself and turned in my tray after I was done and headed back to the barracks. Once there, I put on jeans and a T-shirt and headed down to the common room where a television was located. The furniture was in good shape and I found a couple of guys in there watching the news. After a few hours of watching TV, I headed up to my room, planning on taking a shower and hitting the bed early, as I was quite tired.

When I entered the shower I was alone, but a couple of other guys came in after I had started. I continued to wash while stealing a peek at my barracks mates. They were guys like me; young and in good shape. I didn't stare at them but took a quick peek at the goods and was rewarded with the sight of a couple of fine-looking asses. I left the shower and dried off before heading back to my room. After setting my alarm clock for 0630 hours, I climbed into bed and went to sleep.

I got up, went to breakfast, and was in uniform in the day room by 0800 hours. I was not alone; I counted fourteen other new airmen. Two master sergeants entered the room and began briefing us about the duties performed on the base by the security policemen. If you were assigned to the missile fields, you worked four days on and three days off. If you were assigned to base police, you worked a five-day workweek. The missile security duties required you to stay those entire four days at field locations, traveling from there to the various missile sites.

"Gentlemen, you have arrived here at Warren at a difficult time in world affairs. The new Soviet Union is rattling their vodka glasses all over the place and making plenty of people nervous around the world. We here at Warren, and our other sister missile bases, are the fist that will pound back any aggression from our adversaries that requires nuclear weapons. Because of the tense times we now live in once again, I urge you men to get your shit together as soon as possible. Learn the procedures and security protocols for whatever areas you are assigned to. You men are the ground combat troops of this base. I don't know what the future holds for us, but I know this: No one can top the United States Air Force! No one. Is that clear?"

We all answered, "Yes, Sergeant!"

At the end of the briefing, everyone's name was called out and assigned to a particular security squad known as "flights" in the Air Force. Everyone but me, that is.

"Callahan, you will be assigned to both missile security duties as well as base police duties and therefore you will be assigned to two different flights. See me when this briefing is over."

Everyone turned their heads around to look at me and wonder why I was different. So did I. As I came to find out, because of my graduation status at the top of my squadron, I was being utilized in both capacities here on base just as the first sergeant had told me. I eventually found out that any airman who graduated at the top of their class was assigned to both types of police duty. If nothing else, it would provide a variety of duties for me to perform and alleviate any boredom that builds up from performing repetitive tasks. I also saw distinct career advantages to being trained and experienced in both fields.

"Okay, listen up. I'm now going to assign you to a partner for security duty. As I call out your name, come up front and meet your teammate," the sergeant announced.

"Callahan: Your teammate will be Sergeant Todd Claymore."

As I turned my head, I found myself watching a young sergeant of about twenty-five years of age walk into the room. He was extremely handsome with sandy-colored hair, green eyes, about 6′2″, and looked to weigh about 175 pounds. He had three stripes, which meant he was a "buck sergeant," or the lowest-ranking sergeant in command. He nodded his head to me and shook my hand. I felt my dick twitch in reaction to meeting Sergeant Claymore and thought that maybe being stuck in the field for four days at a time wouldn't be so bad after all.

We were dismissed to join our new partners for lunch and to get acquainted with each other. Once we got our trays of food and sat down at the table, Claymore began to describe what our duties would be.

"First of all, our four days in the field aren't that bad considering we get three days off afterward. We drive out with one other team to our facility where we stay during the tour of duty. The site NCOIC will assign each team to a twelve-hour shift and it's our responsibility to visit each one of our missile sites during the tour of duty. We go out, enter the site, check and make sure everything is secure, and then we leave for the next site. The only change would be if there was an alarm at a particular site, and then we respond to that location. We're going to be doing a lot of traveling by truck, so get used to it. We sleep at the same time so we are rested when we go out. We eat right there at the facility."

"Is there a cook there?"

"No, there will be prepackaged meals that are prepared on base, frozen and then sent out to the field. We nuke 'em and eat 'em. Considering the way we prepare the food, it is surprisingly good. I've never had any complaint with Air Force food."

"Well, that all doesn't sound too bad. Are there weapons on site for us to use?"

"Negative. We go to the base armory and check out weapons. We each get an M16 and a nine-millimeter sidearm and extra ammo. We each have a radio and that's it."

"What are the orders if we find anyone on the site?"

"We shoot to kill. They are classified as national defense sites and deadly force is authorized. Now, if we find a couple of kids on site who just climbed over the fence, then of course we don't shoot 'em. We arrest them and they get turned over to the FBI."

"When do we go out?"

"Tomorrow. Be at the armory at 0600 hours and draw your weapons. Do not chamber a round in the M16. That doesn't happen until we are out in the field and ready to make rounds. Prior to that, the safety remains on, so that all you have to do to fire is flip the safety to single fire or full-automatic fire, and then pull back the charging handle, which as you know puts a round into the chamber. Just like in security police school. Eat breakfast before reporting to the armory. We'll stop for coffee somewhere on the road before we get to our destination. You look a little nervous. Are you?"

"Not really; more excited than anything. I just hope I don't screw up with the codes or anything."

"Just relax and remember your training, that's all. But with everything getting tense over the new Soviet Union, we need to be precise in our code use. If you aren't sure, ask me."

"What happens if I screw up with a code on one of the missile sites?"

"You do not want that to happen! Security control automatically calls a strike in on us, which means that a helicopter full of other security policemen will be dispatched to our location. That is extremely embarrassing and we would both get chewed out by the wing commander, who is a two-star general."

"Oh shit. I hope I don't fuck up."

"Just think before you act, and you'll be fine. By the way, what do you think of the barracks?"

"It's a barracks. At least it's clean and relatively quiet at night. What room are you in?"

"I don't live in the barracks. I moved off base a couple of months ago to my own place. That way, this is more like a regular job than a way of living. Plus, as an NCO, I get extra money to help pay my rent, although it doesn't pay all of it."

"Wow. That's pretty cool. I guess you can have all the girls you want over and no hassle from barracks life, huh? Or are you married?"

"Yeah, well, I get to have a personal life this way and I love it, and no, I'm not married. In time, you can move off base too. You're allowed to live anywhere you want as long as you can report to the base within thirty minutes of a recall order. But you don't make enough yet to be able to afford to make that move. Save your money and then move."

"How long have you been here at Warren?"

"I got here seven months ago. It's not bad considering if I had been assigned to a bomber base, I'd have been humping around an aircraft day or night, and in all weather conditions. Missile duty is for sure the way to go."

"What's next for today?"

"Nothing. We're both off until 0600. Don't forget to bring your toothbrush, and any other personal stuff you'll need, along with extra uniforms and stuff. Most guys just use their duffel bag and that's what I suggest you use. I gotta get going, as I'm meeting someone, so if there isn't anything else, Bryce, I'll see you in the morning."

"Sounds good, Todd."

When he took his tray and walked away from the table, I checked out his impressive-looking ass and once again reminded myself to watch where I looked. I was very careful in basic training and had to continue to be careful now. I got rid of my tray and headed back to the barracks and changed into civilian clothes, which was allowed when not on duty. A couple of the guys asked me if I wanted to go to the movies to catch the matinee and I was happy to say yes.

CHAPTER 2

MY alarm went off at 0500 hours and I jumped out of bed. I had packed my duffel bag and showered before going to bed, so all I had to do was get dressed and eat breakfast. I headed over to the chow hall to eat and returned to the barracks to get my gear. I then headed to the armory and checked out my weapons and loaded them. Todd arrived at the armory by a little before 0600. He got his weapons and then we made one more stop.

At this location, we were issued top secret codes that would be used during our tour of duty. They were only good for us, and each code could only be used once. We were then met by one of the pickup trucks heading out to the field and we were on our way. After about three hours of driving, we stopped for coffee and got right back on the road. In total, it took us a little less than five hours to reach our base of operations. As we approached the gate, two security policemen walked out and motioned for us to exit the vehicle and approach the gate. We had to show our military IDs before we were allowed to return to the truck. Our names were checked against a list of expected personnel to relieve the men on duty and once that was confirmed as correct, the gate was opened electronically and we drove in.

The site consisted of four buildings with nothing that looked out of the ordinary. I had expected something ominous-looking considering what the site represented. After all, it controlled enough destructive power to kill millions of people. We parked, got out of the truck, and entered the main building with our weapons and duffel bags. The old team couldn't wait to be relieved and were already in the truck to go back to base before we had stowed our gear.

We walked into the bunk room where the security teams slept, and everyone threw their hats onto the bed they wanted. Only one team would be sleeping at a time, but we each had our own bed. I took the top bunk over Todd, and stored my uniforms away. It was time for lunch, so we headed into the kitchen area for my first taste of microwaved Air Force food. We went into the freezer and looked at the labels to see what they contained. I chose one labeled "pasta and meat." Todd chose "Salisbury steak," and we tossed the meals into the microwave and set the table. After nine minutes, the distinctive "ding" was heard and we retrieved our food.

I was surprised at how good the food was considering it had been frozen and then subjected to a microwave. We grabbed ice cream for dessert and a soda and headed into the briefing room. We all took seats and reviewed status reports from the outgoing security detail and noted that nothing unusual had occurred.

The NCOIC of the station came into the room and greeted us.

"Okay, men. All of you but one guy has been through this before. You know the drill. Sergeant Claymore, you and Airman Callahan will have the night shift, so I suggest you guys try and get some sleep now. You'll be woken up at 1800 hours, or for you, Callahan, 6:00 p.m. You other two, check your vehicle over and hit the road. Any questions?"

There were none, so we all headed to our respective positions, which meant that Todd and I had to try and sleep after having just eaten. We both got out of our uniforms and hit the bunks in our boxer shorts. It took me at least an hour to get to sleep while Todd appeared to have had no trouble at all.

AT precisely 1800 hours, we were awoken by the gentle voice of the same sergeant who had told us to go to bed. Todd and I each grabbed a towel and headed to the small shower facility. I went in first and was getting used to the water when I turned around to see Todd entering the showers as well. I almost swallowed my tongue in shock.

Not four feet from me stood a man with perhaps the largest dick I had ever seen. Todd was hung about eleven inches, and that was soft! I must have showed a look of awe on my face as Todd noticed my reaction to seeing him naked for the first time.

"Big, isn't it?"

I shook off the feeling of numbness to mumble a response. "Oh, I'm sorry. I didn't mean to stare."

"Don't worry about it; I'm used to it. It's one of the reasons I moved off base, believe it or not. And in case you are wondering, no, it doesn't get any bigger hard; it just kind of wakes up, rises a bit, and looks around."

"Do you get lightheaded when you get hard?" I asked with a smile.

"Oh, I've never heard that one before."

"Sorry. I guess I'm just jealous."

"Why? You look normal to me," he said, staring down at my cock.

I felt myself blush and turned back around facing into the spray from the showerhead.

"Believe me; I've got nothing you should want. Being this big makes it almost impossible to find a bedmate to handle it. People usually just run screaming from me when they get a look. I'd trade it for five inches in a heartbeat!"

"Well, I'd like to see what it was like for just one day!"

"We better get moving. We don't have a lot of time to eat and hit the road."

WE returned to the bunk room and began to get dressed. Todd had a great-looking ass as well as a huge dick. Lucky fuck! We dressed, ate dinner, and headed for the truck after we retrieved our weapons and codes. As we set out from our base location, the sun had just set and we headed to our first missile site. Todd knew the way to all the sites and never referred to a map. After our third site check, I asked.

"How come you don't use a map? You have all the roads and routes memorized?"

"We have to. The last thing we would want is a map in the vehicle with directions to all our missiles. If we were hit, the enemy would have an easy time locating our assets."

"True. How long did it take you to learn the roads?"

"Four months, and I am still a little shaky on a couple of them; but even if we get lost, I know what roads to take to put us right. You need to pay attention to the roads and start to learn them yourself."

"I'll do my best."

"Just study the roads like you were studying my dick in the shower and bunk room, and you'll be fine."

After I finished blushing once more, I said, "I'm sorry about that. It's just I've never seen a guy hung like you before. I didn't mean to make you uncomfortable."

"Forget it. As I said, I'm used to it. Okay, here's another one. You get it this time."

I was more than glad to get the subject off Todd's dick and back onto business. We had arrived at one of the sites, and I got out of the truck with my M16 and opened the gate after entering the secure electronic combination. The gate swung open and Todd drove in, a trigger sensor closing the gate after the truck passed all the way through. I made a perimeter walk of the fencing to make sure that there were no holes in the fence as Todd performed his job with missile control. Once we were comfortable that no one had entered the site without authorization, we radioed in to security control and told them all was secure and exited the site.

This process was repeated until we had checked all the sites in our area of responsibility. We headed back toward our field base, which is known as a launch control facility, with about one hour until daylight. I was tired even though all we did was ride from place to place, and was glad to get back. Todd gassed up the truck from our on-site gas pump so that the next shift would not have to refuel and would be able to hit the road right away.

Before I knew it, our four-day tour of duty was over and we were heading back to the base. We hit the armory to turn in our weapons, and got rid of unused codes at their proper destination.

"Well, that's it for now, Bryce. Would you like to come over for dinner tomorrow night at my place, say around seven?"

Startled, I said yes. He gave me the address, which turned out to be only a five-minute walk after leaving the main base entrance. I then headed to the barracks where I intended to get some sleep. Since we left that morning from the field, neither of us had gotten any sleep that day. While drifting off to sleep, thoughts of Todd and his incredible body filled my mind, making me realize that I was becoming infatuated with the handsome sergeant.

The next day I slept in a bit and missed breakfast. When I did get up, I showered and took another walk around base to get more familiar with everything, realizing that I would be assigned to base police duty sooner or later.

When I returned to the barracks, I went to the dayroom to watch some television and found everyone crowded around a CNN bulletin. I slipped into a chair quietly and tried to ascertain what was happening.

"CNN reports that talks have broken down between NATO and the new Soviet Union on negotiations for a stand-down of all forces that have gone to a higher alert status in recent days. The Soviets are demanding that their former satellite nations be once again absorbed into their union. NATO refuses to even consider such a request as half of the former nations are now members of NATO and have a mutual defense treaty in place. The Soviet premier, Alexandr Popov, refuses to withdraw his demand and states that the West must accede to his demands. He further warns that Poland will be the first nation to be invaded should the Soviet Union be forced to use its military might. Poland reacted to this threat by the Soviets with tremendous anger along with a denouncement of old-style Soviet aggression, with a vow to make it very costly for invading Soviet troops."

The immediate reaction to this announcement by the guys in the room was one of yelling of various favorite obscenities directed at both Popov and the USSR. The room quieted down when the face of President David Windsor of the United States appeared on the screen.

"My fellow Americans: We continue to engage the Soviet Union in dialogue in order to peacefully resolve the tensions between the USSR and the United States. It is my belief that the issues that have arisen are best addressed at the conference table and not the battlefield. NATO is a full partner at these talks and I am hopeful that common sense will prevail and that this crisis will soon pass. In the meantime, I urge all of you listening to my voice not to get overanxious about the current tensions and to go on with your normal lives. We in the government will do all within our power to settle these issues amicably."

As I watched reporters shouting questions to the president's back as he left the White House pressroom, an increased level of tension rose in the room in which I sat. No one talked for a moment as each man began to think what it would be like if we went to war with the Soviet Union. We were responsible for the safety of a giant piece of our nation's nuclear deterrent. It was an awesome responsibility to be placed on the shoulders of men, many of whom were no older than twenty-one. The silence was broken only by the renewed bravado of young men who felt they could never die.

As the day drew on, it was time for me to get ready for my dinner engagement with Todd. I decided to take another shower and put on black 501s, a green polo shirt and sneakers. I checked myself in the full-length mirror that was attached to the back of every barracks-room door in the building. Having passed my own inspection, I proceeded to walk off base to Todd's. I had no problem finding his house and knocked on the door at five minutes to seven.

The door swung open and Todd's voice boomed out. "You're early."

"Hi, Todd. Yeah, I know. Wasn't sure how long it would take me to get to your house."

I entered into a neatly furnished home, which felt lived-in but cared for in a way that spoke well of the owner. Todd told me to sit down and brought me a beer.

"Look, I haven't had time to shower yet; I just got in two minutes before you knocked on the door. I've been out jogging this afternoon and I need to clean up. So, get comfortable, turn on the television if you want, and I'll be just a few minutes."

"No problem. Take your time," I said while checking out Todd's ass as he walked away.

I didn't want to turn on the television and watch more world tension stuff that would only put me out of the mood to have any fun. I could smell a pasta sauce just beginning to heat up on the stove and it smelled wonderful. It seemed like Todd could really cook.

After a couple of minutes, Todd walked out drying his hair. He was naked. His dick was just as huge as it was the last time I saw it. "We're having pasta and salad tonight. I hope that's all right?" he asked, looking up at me.

Once again, I was put off by the beauty of his manhood. I stuttered a response that pasta was fine. My eyes once again admiringly locked onto his dick. He noticed, again.

"You still fascinated by my dick, Bryce?"

"Oh, sorry. I always seem to be saying that to you for staring at your dick. I'll try not to do it again."

He walked toward me, continuing to dry his hair, with his dick swinging to and fro like an elephant as he moved. "Look, it really is okay, I'm not offended." He looked into my eyes and asked the last thing in the world I ever expected to hear from him: "You sure you wouldn't like to take a closer look at it?"

A wave of warmth wash over me from somewhere deep inside my body. I blushed and looked back down to his cock once more. I didn't know what to say. I wanted to do more than look at it again; I wanted to possess it, although I didn't know what the hell I would do with it should that happy event occur. I was also afraid that Todd would freak out if he knew I was gay. Who knew? Would he turn me in?

"Well, you didn't say no, so I take it that means yes. You gay?"

I felt like the deer caught in the proverbial headlights. Since the new president had not had time to repeal the antigay policy of the military, I would be taking a giant risk to be honest with Todd. On the other hand, the behemoth had begun to rise, which told me that Todd was feeling both horny and hopeful of my responding with a "yes."

"Look, Todd, you know as well as I do that they can still throw me out of the Air Force if I was gay and they found out. That's a risk I'm not willing to take for a few minutes' worth of pleasure."

"A few minutes? Hell, you come with me and we might get to eat dinner tonight if we're lucky!"

With that, he turned around and walked through the kitchen into the back of the house. I wiped my sweaty palms off on my jeans, and got up and followed him against my better judgment. I was horny and had been for some time and this was a rare opportunity.

I entered Todd's bedroom with butterflies in my stomach and found him lying naked on the bed with both his hands behind his head. "You're beautiful," was all that I could think to say and felt like a dork after saying it. This was a man clearly more experienced in the realm of sex than was I. I really didn't know what to do.

"Take off your clothes and get in bed, Bryce. Are you a virgin, by any chance?"

"To some things, yes. I have been with guys before."

"Let me guess; your activities were limited to hand jobs and maybe blow jobs?"

"Yeah, and not many blow jobs, actually. Three, to be exact."

I stripped down to my underwear and got onto the bed. In the face of such a large dick, I was intimidated beyond belief with feelings of inadequacy. I lay close to Todd's body and reached out to take his dick in my hand. Before I could make contact, Todd told me to take off my shorts.

Reluctantly, I removed my underwear. Todd was almost twice as big as I was even though I had never had any complaints before. I reached out and took his dick into my hand and played with it to test his former statement that he didn't get any bigger when erect. I slowly jacked him up and down and found that it got firm, but got no bigger.

I was captivated by the length of his dick and the large balls that hung beneath it. After watching me staring at it, he reached over into the nightstand and pulled out a tailor's measuring tape. "Go on, measure it. Everyone wants to see for themselves."

I stretched the cloth tape from one end of his dick to the tip of his head, and found that he was exactly eleven inches long. "I guess it's a damn good thing you don't get any bigger when you're hard, or people really would run screaming from you at the sight of your cock."

"It's bad enough to come close to that. You're so inexperienced, I'm sure all you'll be able to do is jack me off."

I saw that as a challenge and bent over his dick and took him into my mouth as far as I could. He wasn't quite as thick as he could have been, and I was able to get about four inches into my mouth. I began to go up and down on him slowly, working my tongue over the bottom of his shaft, and back over the head. I slowly jacked the inches that I was unable to take as I sucked his dick. The smooth hardness felt wonderful in my mouth even though I could not do his manhood the justice it deserved. I pulled off his dick and ran my tongue down the full length of his shaft and onto his balls. Taking one nut at a time in my mouth, I ran my tongue all over each one. I worked my way back up to the head of his dick and received a compliment for my efforts.

"There might be hope for you yet; that's not half-bad. You say you've only sucked three dicks before?"

"Yeah, I didn't have many opportunities to fool around. One guy wanted to fuck my ass, but I wouldn't let him."

"Oh? Why not?"

"I don't know really. He didn't seem to know what he was doing and I guess I was afraid of the pain involved."

"So, you have a virgin ass."

"Yep, sure do."

"Damn! And you've got a sweet one too. Shame someone isn't gettin' into that."

I smiled, and began to lick his cock once more. I worked my way down the front side of his shaft, around to the underside and back up to the head. I began to once more suck his dick as I moved my mouth up and down on his shaft, varying the speed at which I was sucking. I saw his balls tighten up a bit but wasn't sure what that meant.

He pulled me off his cock and pushed me back onto the bed. Reaching over, he began to play with my dick and balls, which was heaven to me. He moved his mouth down onto my left nipple and began to lightly lick and suck the now awakened protruding nub. This sent small bolts of electricity through my body and increased the hardness of my own erection. He moved to the other nipple and repeated the attention that he had given to my left one.

I began to moan at the incredible feelings he generated within me. I felt as if I was about to melt into a pile of goo that wanted nothing more than to be taken by the man in this bed. While he was sucking on my nipples, he was slowly jacking my average-size cock and I began to feel the early signs of a climax.

"I'm gonna cum if you don't stop that quickly," I warned.

"Oh, you got a ways to go before I let you cum," he said with a chuckle. "The head of my dick needs attention."

I bent over him once again and began to suck him as best I could. I was determined to give him the best blow job I could under the circumstances. Maybe others failed to bring him enough pleasure, but I would do my best to succeed where they had failed. I repeated all the things I had done the first time, but took more time in doing them. My work was rewarded by low moans coming from deep within his throat.

"For not being an experienced cocksucker, you sure are good."

I didn't answer; I just kept working on the object of my desire. I tried to take more of him into my mouth and into my throat but was unable to because of the angle. Todd saw what I was trying to do and offered up a suggestion.

"Here, lay on your back with your head over the edge of the bed."

I shifted around and took the position he suggested, watching as he walked up to me from behind until he stopped directly over my face. As I looked up, I saw a thing of pure beauty. The smooth firm curves of both ass cheeks flowed down until they melded between his legs where his two large balls hung with an even larger cock hanging down. The top of his cock rested on my forehead and all I had to do was move my head a little, open my mouth, and his cock dropped into my mouth.

After I sucked on the end of it for a bit, he once again became firm. He reached down and pulled me farther off the bed so that my head fell back and down, opening the passage of my throat. He reached down and guided his cock into my mouth and pushed forward so that I took at least seven of his inches.

"Just relax your mouth and throat; I'm not going to cut off your air for more than a few moments at a time. Trust me and enjoy it. You're doing great!"

I did as he commanded and felt his cock slide in and out of my mouth. I began to jerk off while he fucked my face and found my excitement level rising by leaps and bounds. The more I was able to take, the faster he pumped in and out of my throat until he began to softly curse at how good it felt.

"Fuck, you listen well. I've had all but about four inches in your mouth which is more than most can handle. Just a little longer, guy, just a little longer," he pleaded.

As his rhythm picked up along with his speed, I felt him push deeper into my mouth and I began to jerk off harder and faster myself. Looking up to see his balls swinging back and forth, it all became too much for me and I began to cum. I groaned and my back arched off the bed. Todd pulled his cock out of my throat and began to jerk off as quickly as I was doing. I shot stream after stream of hot cum all over my face and chest at almost the same time that Todd began to climax. He shot his load down and over my cock and legs until the sheets were wet from his cum.

As we both began to catch our breath, he let his cock drop down and I opened my mouth one more time and sucked his dick in, draining the last drops of his cum into my mouth. I noticed a muscle jerk in his legs as my tongue worked the head of his dick, and he finally pulled out and collapsed on the bed.

"That was incredible! I haven't had that good a blow job for many months now. Are you sure you only went down on three guys before?"

"Yep, that's all. I just got very hot at seeing all your junk swinging over my face and looking at your hot ass while you pumped my mouth and throat."

He got up to bring a towel from the bathroom and began to wipe me off along with himself. When I got off the bed, he pulled the sheets off and threw them into the laundry hamper. He pulled on a pair of shorts and told me to just put on mine and that we would have dinner in our underwear. I wondered at the time if he was counting on a round two after dinner.

"Sit down and I'll get supper on the table. While I'm doing that, tell me about yourself."

"Well, not much to tell really. I grew up with three brothers and one sister, no father in the family, which made money always tight. But one thing I didn't lack was love. We're a close family and I half-expect one of my brothers to join the Air Force also."

"Do they know you're gay?"

"My brothers know, but not my mother or sister."

"Guess there are still some things you keep from a close family, eh?"

"I don't know why I never told them; guess I didn't want to disappoint my mother with the fact that she would have no grandchildren from me. My brothers figured it out as we were growing up. They kept trying to set me up with hot chicks that they had dated, and I kept saying no. They're not stupid. As for my sister, she's so close to my mother that I knew if she found out, it wouldn't be long before my mother knew."

"Did you get any shit from your brothers, or were they supportive?"

"My brothers and I are tight. You fuck with one of us, you fuck with all of us. So, they just took it in stride after a lot of talking about it. They wanted to make sure that I wasn't just afraid of dating or something. Once they realized that I really was gay, they rallied around me. How about you? Any brothers or sisters?"

"Nah, only child, which means I'm kinda spoiled. But my dad was a real bastard; never happy with anything that I did. He always seemed to be disappointed. He wanted me to play football and pushed me hard to join the high school team. The more he pushed, the more I fought against it. Instead, I joined the swim team and excelled at that.

He didn't care because it wasn't what *he* wanted. I joined the Air Force right out of high school just to get away from him."

Todd put the pasta on the table and we ate while chatting more about family and life in general. We talked about how long we both knew we were gay and how difficult it was for Todd to accept it. He talked about dating girls all through high school in order to fit in with the guys but never feeling complete. He also talked about the first time he was with a man; an older man who picked him up in a movie theater when he was sixteen. I talked about my first time, which took place during a Boy Scout camping trip. We took different roads that ended up at the same place for both of us. I got to see a little bit of vulnerability in an otherwise confident and outwardly tough guy.

We killed a bottle of wine with dinner and I helped him clean up when we were finished. Todd said he was ready for dessert and I declined, saying I was full. He smiled at my naivety, took my hand and led me back to the bedroom. I smiled all the way.

"I don't get to enjoy sex very often like I just did with you. Can you blame me for wanting a second round?" he asked with a broad smile and a hard-on that was stretching the hell out of his shorts.

"I'm good for it. You have a very willing student here, so teach me!" I responded with a wink.

We spent the next hour having sex and by the time we were finished, my throat was sore. Todd had a very satisfied look on his face and I was content and tired.

"Look, why don't you spend the night here with me? I've worn you out, and we don't have to be anywhere tomorrow, so you can head back to base after we get up. What do you say?"

"Yeah, I'd like that. I could use a beer if we're gonna watch some television before going to sleep."

"You bet. Beer I got plenty of, and you're welcome to as much as you'd like since you're not going to be walking anywhere tonight. Make yourself at home."

The evening drew to a close with us snuggling on the sofa, beers in hand, watching a John Wayne war movie. I looked over at Todd and really looked at him for the first time. He was a good-looking guy with a heart of gold and the sex drive of a Sultan's harem. The fact that he was fairly decent in the kitchen and the bedroom certainly lent extra appeal to the man.

CHAPTER 3

THE next day we woke up and I took a shower to wash away all the remnants of our love-making sessions, had a cup of coffee, and headed back to base. I had one more day off before it was time to head into the missile fields again.

As I walked, I relived the previous night in my head. The sex had been amazing and the promise to teach me more if I wanted to learn put a smile on my face. Hell yeah, I wanted to learn! The guy was a sex machine even if his equipment was daunting. There was definitely a spring in my step as I showed my ID at the base gate and entered Warren. I knew it was silly, but I felt like I was crushing on the guy after only one night in the sack. The realization that I was both a sex-starved teen and one who was hungry for affection dawned on me. Was Todd the answer to my needs? What could I offer in return?

When I entered the security police barracks, I found most of the guys once again jammed into the dayroom watching CNN. As I stuck my head in, I learned that tensions were not easing between the East and the West. Germany was now warning the Soviets that to invade Poland would cause them to become involved militarily, which opened up old memories of the siege of Stalingrad by the Nazi army.

I headed up to my room to catch a little more sleep when I found a note under my door from the first sergeant's office. I sat on my bunk and opened the envelope, nervous about what I would find.

It was the notification that I was officially classified for base police duty as well as security police duty in the field. It further informed me that Sergeant Todd Claymore would remain my partner for both types of duty as he was also "cross-trained." We would be assigned duties depending upon the needs of the squadron, which simply meant that I would not be sure from one week to the next which type of duty I would be performing.

The letter ended with orders to report to Staff Sergeant Thomas Gray, Base Police Flight Commander, upon return from our next tour of duty in the field. I folded up the letter and put it in my desk. I would show it to Todd the next day when we went back into the field. My thoughts were interrupted by a knock on my door, and when I opened it, I found a messenger from the first sergeant's office ordering me to report to Major Manuel Manchuka, Security Police Commanding Officer, in thirty minutes. The messenger didn't know why, which didn't help me control the feelings in the pit of my stomach. The major didn't send for people unless there was a problem or an issue to be dealt with.

I quickly changed into Class As, the dress blues of the Air Force, and headed over to the major's office, which was within the base police station. The fact that I had not even met my commanding officer before only added to the tension at being summoned to report to him. I walked up to the buck sergeant who controlled access to the CO and told him I was reporting as ordered. He told me to sit down and wait.

In a near panic, I began to run everything through my mind that I might have screwed up, including the entire tour of duty in the field that we had come off two days ago. I had not come up with any problems when I was told to report.

I entered the major's office, stopped four paces from his desk, came to attention, saluted, and stated, "Airman Callahan reporting as ordered, sir."

The major looked up, returned my salute, and said, "At ease.

"First of all, welcome, Airman Callahan, to Warren Air Force Base and to my command. I'm sure you've heard about the level of responsibility that we have upon our shoulders in the security police here, and that you are now a vital part of that responsibility. In light of your graduation status from security police training, you are being promoted to Airman First Class, effective immediately. Here are your new orders effecting that promotion. Further, in looking at your records from tech school, it is noted that you are a good typist and, together with your superior test scores, you are going to fill a need that has come up."

"Yes, sir."

"Sergeant Gray, who you are to report to next week for base police duties, is in need of a desk sergeant for his flight. I'm going to make an exception in your case and give you a try in that post. Usually the post has a buck sergeant or higher in that position, but all of his men have ten thumbs and can't type worth a damn. There are many reports that have to be typed and are integral to maintaining a valid record of incidents. If you do well in that position, you will be assigned to those duties permanently. How do you feel about that, Callahan?"

"Sir, I'm more than willing to perform those duties and execute the post orders to the best of my ability, sir. I appreciate your confidence in me, Major, and I won't let you down."

"Very well. I will inform Sergeant Gray that you have accepted the position. Now, if you turn out to be a fuckup, then you're out of that job, and on the streets in a patrol car or standing guard duty at the base gates. Clear?"

"Yes, sir."

"Very well. Dismissed."

I saluted once again, executed a perfect about-face, and exited the major's office. I was floating on cloud nine for a second time that day. While I wasn't really sure what a "desk sergeant" did, the major had said that it was a special duty. As I left the major's office, I had to walk past the desk sergeant area and noted that the sergeant on duty sat behind bullet-proof glass, on a raised platform. If I were to stand directly in front of the desk area, my head would come just above a shelf that stuck out from the bottom area of the central pane of glass. There was a hole for talking, and a tray for passing paperwork underneath to the man on duty. To the left of that window was a door with a code lock on it that controlled access to the desk area.

I left the building and headed back to the barracks. I was sure that I would get a full briefing from Todd about what duties I would be performing since we were going back into the field the next morning. I liked the fact that Todd would come with me to base police duties as well.

THE next morning, I reported to the armory at 0545 hours and checked out my weapons. Todd showed up a couple minutes after me and did the same thing. The other team that was going out with us had the truck and we stopped next at the code room and retrieved our codes for that tour of duty.

Todd was quiet and appeared to be very tired. Once we were in possession of our codes, he went to sleep in the backseat of the vehicle while we traveled out to our field base of operations. The ride was long and boring and even stopping for coffee didn't help much. The land in Wyoming becomes rather flat and dull along the urban highways and it wasn't until we traveled into the more mountainous regions that color and form began to break up the landscape.

After our arrival, we went through the same procedures to gain access as we had the first time. Once again, the team we were relieving couldn't wait to get out of there and back to base for their three-day break.

"Bryce, you okay with the night shift again if the sarge wants us to take it?"

"Sure. There's less traffic on the roads and the weather is nice."

As expected, we were told that we would have the night shift unless we objected. We didn't, so we hit the sack without eating this time. I found it hard to eat and then try to sleep, so we passed on lunch. I didn't bring up our activities over the break as I figured this wasn't the time or place to discuss our personal lives. We got out of our uniforms, and after Todd smiled at me, got into our bunks and went to sleep.

We woke up, showered, dressed, and had dinner. This time I had stuffed cabbage, which was surprisingly good. Todd had some kind of fish, which I can't stand, so we were both happy. We loaded up a thermos full of coffee and headed to our truck.

Just as the first time, Todd knew exactly where we were going to check on our "babies." But after only about ten minutes on the road, security control radioed us that there was an alarm at missile site Bravo 49, which required us to deviate and respond immediately. Since most of our driving was done on back roads, there was very little traffic and we traveled at nearly 75 miles per hour en route to the alarm. Things were going great and we were making good time until we rounded a road and almost ran headlong into a steer that had gotten out of its pasture. Todd swerved; we went off the road and up an embankment before coming to a stop.

"Fuck! That was close. If I hadn't missed that walking pot roast, he would have caved in the entire front end of the truck and we would more than likely be injured right now."

"I'll jump out and take a quick look around the truck to make sure we didn't bust anything loose," I offered.

A quick inspection revealed no damage and we were back on the road heading to the alarm at a slower pace. After ten more minutes Todd slowed the truck down and said we were near the site. It was just dusk, and he cut the headlights off so that we wouldn't be as noticeable coming from the roadway, turning onto a side road that led to the site.

As we approached, I could see no vehicles of any kind but still could not see the site itself. "Security control, this is security one. We've arrived on site. Stand by for a sit rep," I said into the mic. Security control acknowledged my message, waiting for the situation report that would tell them if we had a real problem or not.

We parked about a hundred feet from the site and dismounted our vehicle. Todd walked toward the site on one side of the road and I took the other. We drew near enough to tell that no one was present inside the fence, which allowed me to begin breathing again. Todd signaled for me to take cover behind a large rock and give cover for his final approach.

I flipped the safety off and selected single fire on my M16 and scanned the surrounding terrain for anyone hidden in the brush or lying on the ground. When Todd got to the gate, he entered the code and went on site. After another minute, he signaled me to join him on the launch site. We walked the fence line looking for holes or other signs that tampering had taken place and found nothing. I was about to tell him that everything looked secure when I heard the very distinct sound of a rattle, signaling the presence of one of the numerous rattlesnakes that dotted the terrain where our sites were located.

I looked down at an adult rattler coiled and ready to strike. Before I could react and warn Todd that there were snakes on site, it struck my leg just above the ankle. I screamed like a schoolgirl, jumped and flipped the fire selector over to full automatic and opened up on the snake. Before I could take my finger off of the trigger, fifteen rounds were fired in just over one second. Todd yelled and hit the ground thinking that we were under attack. The snake all but disintegrated from the powerful bursts of my weapon.

Todd came running over to see what I had just fired on and was dumbstruck to find what was left of the snake. While he was ranting at me over discharging my weapon, I was examining my leg to see if the snake had penetrated my combat boot, which rose about six inches above the ankle. I was relieved to find that while there were signs that the inside of the boot had the beginnings of two punctures, the fangs had not managed to strike flesh.

"God bless whoever invented combat boots!" I said with immense relief. I hated snakes. I hated snakes more than almost anything else in the world and now I had a real reason to hate them. One had just tried to kill me.

"Are you okay? Did you get bit?" Todd asked with genuine concern.

"No, but if it had struck any harder, I would have venom in me right now. I imagine this is what set off the intrusion alarm, wouldn't you?"

"Yeah, more than likely. I need to call this in right away. I'll use the secure phone to do it; you change magazines so that you have a full load in the clip. Then get the truck and drive it up here."

I knew it was a big deal if we discharged any of our weapons for any reason. There was now a ton of paperwork to fill out, and command had to be notified by security control. I really didn't have a choice but to shoot the damn thing. I hoped it wouldn't get me in trouble with the major after having just been given a choice assignment.

After finishing our check of the site, we left to finish our rounds. We would have to do the reports when we got off duty, which meant less sleep and relaxation. The rest of the night went as normal as one could hope. There were no further alarms or incidents of any kind. We got back to our field base as the sun began its daily rise in the east. I gassed up the truck for the day shift and headed inside, where we found the NCOIC of the station waiting for us.

"Okay, what the fuck happened out there on Bravo Forty-Nine?" asked the irritated sergeant.

"Basically, Sergeant, I stepped on a rattlesnake in the dim light on the site, and it struck my leg. I jumped back and shot it before it could strike again. It was pure reflex on my part and the snake is definitely dead."

"Well, you may have to report to the CO when you get back to base. No one likes a report of a weapons discharge because everyone and their grandmother have to be notified. You opened up with an M16 inside the secured area of an ICBM, which makes it a "nuclear incident." A report will be at the Pentagon by this time tomorrow. Fill out all the reports, turn them in to me for review and then hit the sack."

As we were getting ready to sleep, Todd looked over at me and said, "Don't let it worry you. It was a justified use of your weapon and that's how the reports will read. Don't let that old bull of a sergeant in there scare you. Get some sleep before we have to do it all over again tonight."

It took me almost ten minutes before I could shut my mind down in order to sleep. I kept replaying the incident over in my head. There really wasn't anything I could have done differently.

The tour of duty was over and we arrived back on base in late afternoon where I found a note at the armory telling me to report to the CO first thing in the morning. My guts tightened up and a mild feeling of fear crept into my heart. Damn, there was nothing else I could have done! What did they want me to do? Just let those stinking snakes bite and do nothing? Todd once again reassured me that it was routine. The CO had to talk to me so that he could report to his bosses that he had talked to me. Weapons discharge really was a big deal.

I parted ways from Todd with no plans to get together as we were both to report to base police for duty after a one-day break. We both would be catching up on some sleep and getting our uniforms ready for this duty. We wore Air Force blues for base patrol and not the green army-type fatigues. Our leather gear also had to be highly shined along with badges and belt buckles. We were, after all, the elite of the Air Force ground combat troops. In fact, we even wore distinctive red berets for base police duty.

After grabbing dinner and getting my uniforms ready, I hit the sack after watching more news on the world situation. In reports from the Soviet Union, it seemed like the old-style hard-line Stalinists were back in power, and that wasn't good for anyone. After all, Stalin had murdered more than twenty million of his own citizens in his climb to, and maintaining of, his power to rule the Soviet Union.

The next morning I got up, showered, and dressed, but didn't go to breakfast. I had butterflies the size of pterosaurs. I sat in my room until ten minutes before my appointment and left for the base police building where the CO maintained an office. The same aide was sitting at the desk and when I stopped in front of him, he just looked at me and smiled.

"Glad to see you're unarmed, Callahan," the base comedian said.

"Funny. I'm reporting as ordered."

"He told me to send you right in when you got here. So, knock on the doorjamb, and report."

"Enter," was the reply to my knock. I stood before the major's desk and reported as I had just a short time ago. When he looked up, I saluted and he returned my salute.

"Callahan, I have here the reports on your discharge of your M16, including a supplemental report from Sergeant Claymore. Do you have anything to add to the official reports of the incident?"

"No, sir. Everything in the report is just as it happened."

"Can you look at me and tell me you had no other choice but to fire fifteen rounds of ammo into that snake?"

"Sir, I had no other choice. The rattler struck me once and was coiling back to strike me again. He hit my boot the first time, but I was afraid he would go higher on the second strike, sir."

"Very well. Then I consider the matter closed, and will classify it as a justified use of a weapon in order to defend your life. Hopefully, you won't run into any snakes while manning the desk here in this building or I fear there wouldn't be much left when you were done shooting!" he said with a smile.

"Yes, sir. I hope I never run into another snake anywhere."

"You understand when to report to Sergeant Gray for your new duties?"

"Yes sir, tomorrow night at twenty-two hundred hours for guard mount. I'm looking forward to the job, sir, and I appreciate the opportunity."

"I have confidence in you, Callahan, and know you'll do a good job for Sergeant Gray. That's all. You're dismissed."

I saluted and left the office. On the way out, I smiled at the aide at the desk. He almost looked disappointed that he didn't get to hear me being chewed out and I wanted to give him the finger, but resisted the urge.

I was now starving but had missed breakfast hours so I would have to wait until lunch. When I returned to the barracks, I found Todd waiting in my room, sitting at my desk with a look of concern on his face.

"Well, what happened? Are you okay?"

"Great to see you, Todd. Yeah, I'm fine. He just asked me if I had another choice besides firing, and I told him no. As far as he is concerned, the matter is closed. He asked me if I understood when to report to Sergeant Gray, and I said yes, and that was it."

"Good. I felt fairly certain that you were out of the woods on this, but you never know. It is the military, after all, and the Pentagon was in on the deal. Look, you got any plans for the rest of today?"

"Not really. I figure like in the field, we'll have to sleep tomorrow during the day, so we can stay awake all night long. Whatcha got in mind?"

Todd smiled and looked down my body. "My car is here. Why don't you change, throw your personal stuff into a bag, and spend the rest of today and tonight at my place? I'll cook us dinner again and get some beer. Interested?"

"I don't know. It isn't fair for you to be buying the food all the time for us, and I can't afford to help right now. I don't have any way to pay you back," I replied, looking as innocent as I could pull off.

"Oh, you'll pay for dinner, don't you worry about that. And you won't need any money. Come on. Change and let's get out of here; this place gives me hives."

Todd watched closely as I changed into shorts, T-shirt, and sneakers. I threw my toothbrush, comb, and a change of underwear into a small bag and we were gone. As we rode back to his place, I asked, "Can you drop me off on base tomorrow evening, early? I want to make sure my uniform is perfect for my first appearance at base police."

"Yeah, no problem. While you are learning desk duties, I'll be on patrol. I'll probably have Police Four assigned to me. Police Four, as you will learn, is your general call car for any routine calls you receive at the desk. Sergeant Gray will have Police Three, the duty officer, who is a second lieutenant, will have Police Two, if we even see anything of him, and God forbid, the CO has Police One should he have to come out for some reason. There more than likely will also be a Police Five, which will give you three cars for incidents. Security control also has three security trucks on patrol in the restricted zones and they can be borrowed if the shit hits the fan."

As he finished his little briefing, we arrived at his place. When we got out of the car, he popped the trunk and pulled out groceries that he had bought on the way to pick me up on base. He sat them on the kitchen table and headed to his room to change into shorts. I began to pull things out of the bags so they could be put away. Midway down in the second bag, I found a box of rubbers and a very large tube of lube. I smiled and put them back so he didn't know I had found them.

"You didn't have to start doing that. Get a beer and go sit down and relax; it's our day off."

"Well, if you insist," I replied with a smile. "What's for dinner anyway?"

"I got us a couple of steaks for the grill, some corn on the cob, and baked beans and coleslaw. You like?"

"Oh hell yeah, I like."

After he put everything away, he grabbed a beer and sat down on the sofa next to me and put the television on. "Do you plan on visiting the gay bar here in Cheyenne anytime? 'Cause if you do, you better be careful: the place gets staked out by the Office of Special Investigations every once in a while. They like their occasional witch hunts and there is no better fun for them than huntin' queers."

"Well, I'm sure President Windsor will be repealing all that 'don't ask, don't tell' bullshit in the near future. They better do their huntin' while they can. But to answer your question, no, I had no plans on going out to the bar or trying to hook up with anyone. Why do you ask?"

"Oh, I was just curious, that's all. I kinda like you, and you're easy on the eyes."

"Well, that's sweet. Thank you. I like you also and you're hard on the eyes, but not in the looks department, just the dick department," I said with a laugh. "Besides, I always seemed to fall for my teachers in high school, and you did say you were teaching me things."

"Oh yeah, I'm gonna teach you a few things if you want to learn."

"You're thinking about my ass cherry, arn'cha?"

"Now why would I do that? Sir, you have mistaken me for a wanton hussy who only wants one thing!"

When I stopped laughing, I looked at him, and leaned over and stole a kiss. It was just after noon, but I smelled cologne on the man. "Look, you are a man, a horny young man, and yes, I know what you want. If you're nice, you might get a crack at it, but I can't promise you anything. I know I'm not the first one to tell you that your size frightens me when I think about you wanting to stick that thing up my ass. I can almost feel my asshole pucker shut!"

It was Todd's turn to laugh out loud and lean over to me for a kiss. I put my hand around the back of his head and held him longer than he was planning while we played dueling tongues. I might not know anything about fucking, but I sure knew about kissing.

When I let him go from the kiss, he looked at me and smiled with a twinkle in his eyes. The last time I noticed that in a guy, he managed to talk me into bed for the first time. Since Todd had already passed that goal, I could only imagine what he was thinking.

We had a couple more beers, and then he threw the steaks on the grill, and I shucked the corn and got the water boiling. We sat down around seven to eat, and the food was fantastic. The food on base was good, but nothing compared to steaks on the grill, corn on the cob, and a handsome man to eat it all with.

We cleaned up and sat back down to watch a movie. It was Mel Gibson in one of his cop movies and we enjoyed the give-and-take between Gibson and Danny Glover. Toward the end of the movie, Todd put his arm around my shoulder and I sank into his solid chest. It felt right, but it was far more than any potential bedroom action that made me content; it was the closeness with another man. I was a guy who needed affection in my private life and Todd showed no signs of being afraid of expressing that. I ate it up like a puppy dog with its first bowl of puppy chow.

When the movie ended, he bent down and kissed me warmly. I smiled and he flicked the television off with the remote. "Well, it's after ten and here's what I suggest: we lay down for an hour or so and get some sleep. We wake up about one, get up, shower and find something to occupy our time. We need to be able to sleep in the daytime tomorrow so we can report for third shift tomorrow night."

"Okay. Sounds like a plan. But are we able to just go to bed and sleep for an hour or two?" I asked with a smile.

"What do you think we'll occupy some of our time with after sleeping?"

I laughed and we got up and went into the bedroom, took off all our clothes and jumped into bed. I snuggled up to Todd and he put his arm around me and we fell asleep. By the time we woke up, it was actually three o'clock, which was way past when Todd thought we should be back up.

"Okay. You jump in the shower, and I'll put some coffee on."

I was done washing and turned the water off and opened the shower curtain to find Todd sitting there waiting for me with a towel in his hands. His gaze fell down my body and came back up. I smiled at the obvious appraisal of my body that he was engaged in. So, I played along and did a slow turn while standing in the tub so he could once again check out my ass. He threw me the towel and gave me his hand to lean on while I got out. He stripped his shorts off and slapped me on the ass as he turned the water back on and got into the shower himself.

I dried myself off and brushed my hair, which was longer now that I had gotten rid of that "just out of boot camp" look. I heard the water turn off and it was my turn to quickly sit down with Todd's towel in my hands and when he opened the curtain, I looked his body over. My breath still caught in my throat upon seeing his long dick and low-hanging balls, which were quite relaxed from the hot water. He was just so damn big; I couldn't help but stare again. Todd then did his own turn in the bathtub and I was able to admire his bubble butt again. It was a thing of beauty.

He got out and took the towel from me and quickly dried off. "Just wrap the towel around you and let's have our coffee before fun and games, okay?"

"Sounds good to me. Why bother with the towels, though?"

"Nosy neighbors. All I need is for them to be peeking into my windows and see us cavorting around in the nude. Next thing you know, they're calling the base. As long as they don't see anything, we're fine."

We sat at the breakfast bar in his kitchen and sipped a really good cup of coffee. He used imported coffee from Hawaii, called Kona roast, which had an incredible flavor and cost about $26 a pound. He saw the expression on my face and said, "I only use the best for special company."

I blushed and said, "I bet you tell that to all your tricks."

"Ha! As I told you, it's been some time since I last got laid. I was about to begin chewing the paint off of the walls when you came along."

"Well, let me ask you then: Why didn't you go to the bar, or advertise on the Internet? After all, there is no shortage of gay men in the area, I'm sure."

"For the same reason that I advised you against going to the bar: OSI. They don't care how much money the Air Force loses by discharging a man for being gay. They would wipe out the base if they found that everyone was gay. We merely replaced the witches from Salem, that's all. Besides, you're damn cute, and you know it. Your ass makes me think of all kinds of evil things," he said with a bright smile.

On that note, I finished my coffee and made a big show of putting it down on the counter empty. I was now horny as hell at the thought of what he might show me in the way of new delights tonight. He drained his cup and we went into the bedroom once again.

He peeled off his towel and I did the same. We stood staring at each other; me with a little trepidation. "You *are* going to be very careful with me, right?"

"Of course. The last thing I want is to hurt you because then you will be too frightened to ever try it again. If I do things right, you will enjoy yourself and want more."

I got on the bed and lay down on my side and Todd joined me. He took me in his arms and kissed me deeply while running his hand over my shoulders, down my back and up again. I moved my hand over his chest, tweaking his nipple as I went. This got a moan from him and when I broke the kiss, I traveled to that nipple and gently sucked and tongued the bud. I moved to the other one and gave it the same attention.

I pushed him flat on his back and moved my lips down his body toward his cock. I wanted to get him as excited as I could so that if he managed to penetrate me, he would cum fairly quickly. I knew I couldn't take a long fucking as I had never been done that way before.

Once again, I struggled to get my mouth around his dick and worked it as best I could. I played with his balls while sucking and was rewarded with the sounds of pleasure emanating from his throat. He moved his hand down over my ass, squeezing each cheek as he went. After a short while, he pulled me off his cock and back up to his face.

"Don't get too carried away down there, or I won't be able to introduce you to an entirely new world of sexual enjoyment!"

I had to laugh, and said, "That was kinda my idea."

"Bryce, I promise I will be gentle. Don't ya think I have my technique down? Otherwise, I would never get to fuck a guy, at least not more than once."

"Okay. I trust you, but stop if I say stop, okay?"

"Agreed."

It was his turn to work his way down my body but he didn't take as much time getting to my dick as I did to him. Before I knew it, he had taken me in his mouth and worked up and down the entire length of my shaft. Between his sucking and the gentle breeze blowing down on us from the ceiling fan, I was in heaven. I had blow jobs before and even one from Todd, but this was even more enjoyable than I remembered. God, I loved sex!

When he stopped, he rolled me over onto my stomach. I immediately tensed up and he saw my ass cheeks clench. "Relax; I'm nowhere near being ready to enter you."

I did as he told me to, and I felt him spread my ass cheeks with his hands and then the feeling of his tongue hitting that spot. I saw sparks and grabbed the pillows as I tried to control my reaction to Todd eating my ass. My toes curled and a gasp escaped my throat. "Fuck, that's fucking great! Where did you fucking learn to do that?"

"Just be quiet and enjoy."

As I experienced the tongue action I was getting, my mind had trouble formulating thoughts on how much I liked what he was doing to me. It felt almost as good as the climax itself and I was now in an extreme state of heat. This went on for almost a half-hour until he finally stopped. I heard him open the draw of the nightstand and looked to see him pull out a tube of lube and a rubber. He squirted lube onto his fingers and began to work one into my ass. I pushed back to meet the thrust of his finger and was quite into the feeling when he put a second finger in. It just felt even better and I continued to enjoy the finger fucking.

"Doesn't this feel good?"

"Oh hell yeah, it feels good. Keep it up!" I urged.

Todd inserted a third finger and I found that I was rather loose from him eating my ass, and assumed that was the purpose of the long, thorough oral work. After a while, I heard him rip open the rubber package and even though I was relaxed and very sexed up, I began to tense. He immediately inserted a finger back into me and I once again welcomed the invasion.

"Now, when I begin to push, just relax. Don't fight it; just let me enter you. I will stop once I feel my head pop through your entryway. I will stop every inch or so, until you are used to my dick. If it hurts, just say so, and I will stop. But, don't tense up; just force yourself to relax."

I began to breathe in and out slowly and forced my mind off of my ass and onto the feel of the headboard that I had my hands up against. Todd rolled me over so that we were looking at each other, and pulled my legs up and over his shoulders. He pulled my torso down toward him so that my ass was lined up against his dick. He pushed the head of his dick into my opening ever so slightly and told me to keep relaxing, and to remember the oral treatment he had just given me.

I was well-lubed and his pressure made my opening give way. Once he slid in, he stopped as he had promised. It hurt only a little bit and I told him to go on. He leaned over my chest and looked down into my eyes as he pushed a little bit farther. When he saw my face show the signs of my reaction to the thicker part of his dick, he stopped again and once again told me to relax and keep breathing.

I did as I was told and he continued to push inward. I felt myself filling up with the length and width of his unusual cock and after he said he had about nine inches in me, I began to panic. "Look, I'm not sure about this. The pain is rather intense. You better stop."

He stopped at once but instead of pulling out, which is what I had in mind, he bent down farther and kissed me. The pain eased and I got lost in his kiss. I ran my hands over his back as we continued to kiss and before I knew it, he was all the way in me. All eleven inches of Todd were now buried deep inside my ass. I relaxed as much as I could, and realized that there was no pain any longer. I smiled up at Todd and he knew what that meant.

He began to pull out and push back in with short strokes, not intending to pull almost all the way out and slam it back in. He was using nice short strokes and I began to really enjoy it when my prostate gland woke up and shot feelings through me that I had never experienced before. My own dick, which had been flaccid, became rock-hard and throbbed each time his cock ran over my prostate. Before I knew it, I was saying the last thing I thought I would ever say to Todd: "Fuck me harder; show me what it's like!"

Much to Todd's credit, he did no such thing. He did, however, pull about halfway out and move back in with a regular rhythm, establishing a nice slow-paced fucking that I really was enjoying. He kissed me from time to time as he fucked me but always continued to stare down into my eyes. God, he had beautiful eyes and I became lost in them as the pleasure I was feeling became more intense. After about twenty minutes of fucking, I began to feel slightly less pleasure and a hint of discomfort due to the lube drying out. Todd could tell from my face that it was becoming less enjoyable for me and rather than stop, lube up again, and reenter me, he picked up the pace as he was near climax.

I knew he was trying to finish and held on for the ride. As he moved faster and faster, he threw his head back and began to groan. His climax quickly built and exploded all at once, as he shot stream after stream of hot cum deep into my ass. When he had finished cumming, he collapsed on my chest and our sweat mingled together. I kissed him on his neck and held on as his breathing began to return to normal.

Finally, he moved up, pulled out of my ass and removed the now-filled rubber and threw it in the wastebasket next to the bed. He collapsed onto his back with the audible "thwap" of his cock hitting his stomach.

"Oh, boy did you do well! I haven't been able to enjoy a fuck like that in at least five years. You're something else for being a virgin!"

"Well, a lot had to do with the way you got me all hot and bothered with the oral part. I think I was ready for a telephone pole after you finished phase one on my ass," I said with a smile. "I really did enjoy that; you know what you're doing, mister."

"Thank you. Now let me take care of you," he said while looking at my now-soft dick.

"Actually, I'm good. Just let me enjoy what you just did. Maybe in the morning, you can jack me off."

"Deal. I'm beat after all that; let's go to sleep."

We once again snuggled as we fell asleep, but I noticed that he held me even closer than he had before. In no time, he was fast asleep and I began to drift off with a rather proud feeling that I could take him and give him so much pleasure.

CHAPTER 4

THE next morning, we woke up, showered, and had breakfast. Todd dropped me off at base. My ass was sore as hell and I had to sit easy for a bit until I got used to it. By mid-afternoon, I was back to normal after another long hot shower.

I tried to get some sleep so that I would be able to stay awake all night, but only managed to get about another two hours of rest. I got up around 1700 hours, threw on some jeans, and hit the chow hall for dinner. I was due to report to the base police building for guard mount at a little before 2200 hours but had to draw my 9 mm sidearm before then, which meant I had to be at the armory no later than 2145 hours. Guard mount was still a phrase I had to get used to hearing. It meant that we would have to line up and stand at attention while we were inspected to ensure that we were properly dressed for duty. This was also when everyone got their assignments for that shift. We worked an eight-hour shift on base police, which meant we would be off at 0600 hours.

At 2130 hours, I was dressed in the appropriate uniform, leather gear for my weapon, extra ammo clips, handcuffs, and badge hanging from my left breast-pocket button. The last thing was to put on a beret, and I was ready. I smiled when I took one last look in the mirror; damn, but I was hot-looking in uniform! I smiled all the way out of the barracks as I headed to the armory to draw my weapon and get over to base police.

I didn't see Todd until I reported for duty to Sergeant Gray, the flight commander of the group I was now assigned to. It was Gray's opinion that I could not be a desk sergeant without having been on base patrol to know where everything was located. One of the duties of a desk sergeant was to dispatch patrol cars to incidents. I would be assigned to Police Four for the next two weeks in order to learn the base.

Guard mount was called to order and everyone fell into place. We stood at attention as both Sergeant Gray and the duty lieutenant inspected each man for appearance and proper equipment. Not one thing was found wrong with any of the men, and the duty officer departed the station for whatever the duty officer did. No one really knew, except that he showed up from time to time to cause trouble.

"Okay. You all have your assignments; hit the road. Police Four, you'll be gate relief tonight so the men on the main gate can eat."

I introduced myself to Airman First Class Donald Baxter, who I would be riding with for at least tonight. We exchanged pleasantries as we checked out our patrol car, making sure there was no damage anywhere on the vehicle before we took responsibility for it. This was a ritual that every man who took possession of an Air Force vehicle was required to do. We also checked it over at the end of the shift to make sure that no damage had been picked up during the shift.

As we hit the road, Baxter told me it was his job to help me learn the base layout so that I could take over desk duty within two weeks. This meant that we drove to every remote corner of the base as well as to all the barracks, businesses, and base housing. The last part included identification of the houses of the wing commander, his assistant, the base commander and his assistant, and one or two other significant residences. We had a resident two-star general on base as wing commander. The wing commander was responsible for the operation of the entire mission of the base, which included the missiles in the field.

The base commander was only responsible for the smooth operation of the base itself, and dealt with most of the discipline problems that rose to that level of review.

The base also had a full hospital; a cemetery dating from World War II, with German POWs interred; a golf course; and tons of restricted zones that no one without the proper clearances could enter. That very first night, I found out what the job of main base guard encompassed. At 0200 hours, Baxter and I relieved the two base police officers who stood guard at the main gate. After 1800 hours, the main gate was the only gate open for entrance or exit from the base. During the daylight hours, there were three gates that could be used.

We waived in cars that carried the correct stickers on the bumper, and saluted all blue stickers as that meant it was an officer's car. Any car not displaying the proper sticker was halted and identification was sought from the occupants. If they produced military ID, they were allowed to proceed onto base. If they were civilians seeking entry to visit someone, they had to pull over and be met and escorted by the military member.

These were the procedures during Def Con Three, which was the lowest our base was ever classified. The rest of the military was at Def Con Four during normal times, but Air Force nuclear forces were always one level higher in alert status. The lower the number of the defense condition went, the higher tensions were in the world. If the defense condition ever went to Def Con One, it meant we were at war, which included the use of the nukes.

The next two weeks went swiftly and I learned the layout of Warren Air Force Base well. Sergeant Gray tested me on my knowledge of the base, and in particular the sensitive areas of the base. When I passed, I was assigned to the position of desk sergeant as scheduled.

Todd and I had been seeing each other both on and off duty. We were getting together for dinner twice a week and sex at least once a week. He was continuing to teach me all the tricks in the book when it came to sex and I was becoming quite experienced. It was now a lot easier for me to accommodate Todd's sexual equipment and the level of enjoyment with our sexual escapades continued to rise for both of us. We were now very comfortable in each other's company as well as each other's arms. I felt good when I was with him and felt the beginning of feelings for him, which concerned me a little bit.

It was my first night of duty as desk sergeant. I was a little nervous and, being that I now had a roommate assigned to my room, getting dressed was a little more complicated. My roommate was assigned to field security duty, as I had been upon arrival. He was on a three-day break, which in his case meant a three-day party. When I was finally satisfied with my appearance, I left for the armory after having kisses blown to me by Dustin the irritating roommate.

We assembled for guard mount and everyone got their assignments. As expected, I was assigned to desk sergeant duty with the outgoing man, who was being transferred to security duty in the Middle East. I had exactly two weeks to learn the ropes of the desk; although Sergeant Gray would spend a lot of time in the beginning with me also.

The first order of business was for the rookie, meaning me, to make the coffee. Once that was done, I took my seat next to Sergeant Lemoyne and we began my on-the-job training.

"The most important thing to remember is this: for every situation, there is an SOP. SOP stands for standard operating procedure. You reach up here over the desk and bring down one of these large black binders depending on the nature of the incident. You open it, find the particular situation, and follow the directives contained within. This makes it easy on you as you don't have to make any major decisions;

just implement. On major incidents, there will also be a call list for you to notify. You contact every number on the list and brief the officer on the situation. On some incidents, you will be calling everyone from the wing commander on down the line. Any questions so far?"

"No, that's pretty clear."

"Okay, the phone is self-explanatory. When the phone rings, you will see one of the buttons light up and all you have to do is read the button to see who's calling. Unless the call is coming from off base, or from a barracks, you will know the origin of all major calls before you pick up the phone. These lines here will have officers on the other end every time the phone rings," he said as he pointed to various buttons. "These buttons are the phones at the various base gates. They are labeled one, two, and three. That is obviously Gate One, the main front gate; Gate Two is the western gate that is open only during daylight hours, and Gate Three is the back gate, also only open during daylight hours. For most major incidents, you will order the base sealed by notifying any open gate to shut down traffic, both incoming and outgoing, depending on the nature of the incident.

"For example, a robbery alarm from the base NCO club would require you to shut down all traffic leaving the base. What the gate guys need to be careful of is, if there is a fleeing vehicle, that the car simply does not swing over and go out the inbound side of the gate.

"Over here is the base alarm panel. All of these lights and buttons are for a different alarm at each location. Some of these alarms go to secure, highly secret classified facilities. You need to know what to do immediately without looking it up. Once you initiate the first actions, you can pull the book down to make sure you didn't forget anything.

"You will get calls occasionally from the CO, who might give you a phone number of where to reach him all night. When he does that, he's at his girlfriend's house, but you never tell that to anyone asking where he's at. He is married, for one thing. If someone like the wing commander walks in here and demands to know where he is, you simply say you have a phone number for him and offer to get him on the phone for the general."

"Wow, there's a lot to this job. What about paperwork?"

"At the start of each shift, like I've done here, you begin a shift report. Everything that happens goes into the report. Now that it is computerized, typos will not be accepted. For many incidents, a separate report must be prepared. For example, if someone gets assaulted, you have to initiate a 'crimes against persons' report. The reports must be without error, as it could go all the way to the top. You put one copy, the original, into the CO's box; Sergeant Gray gets a copy; and the final copy goes into this book. This includes all supplemental reports as well.

"Now as for the radio: when a call comes in, you send Police Four on all routine calls, and if we have a Police Five, you send him also if backup is warranted. Police Three, as you know, is Sergeant Gray or whoever is acting as the flight commander. He can roll on any call he chooses. You dispatch Police Three to any major incident or any incident that involves an officer at the full colonel level or above."

"So some shifts, we only have two cars on the road; Police Three and Four?"

"Correct. It depends on who's on leave, off sick, or assigned to some kind of special duty for that shift. The full complement is three cars, and two men on the main gate. On day shift, one man is assigned to each of the other two gates. We also usually have a third man on the main gate who handles visitor control. Any person or vehicle that is not military must be diverted to the visitor control building where that airman makes sure they are escorted by a military member. This extra man also has a patrol car at the gate and can be dispatched on a call if more men are needed, and then he would be Police Six. He also provides breaks for the other two gates when they are open, and one of the main gate guys handles visitor issues while he is gone.

"Now, we are police control. You can reach security control via the phone, or radio. Security control has three vehicles that patrol the secured section of the base. In an emergency, you can request assistance from security control and, in some types of incidents, they are automatically dispatched to back up base police. So, if all hell breaks loose, you could have as many as six vehicles. The security patrols have two men in each vehicle."

"What kind of incident would bring in security units?"

"One example would be an alarm from the Plans and Intelligence vault. Everyone rolls on that alarm because of what's contained at that location."

"What is contained there?"

"All of our security codes that are issued to the guys who go into the field, classified reports, maps, codes, and things like that. It requires a maximum response from us. There are a couple of other locations like that and you will come across them when you study the SOP books before taking over by yourself. The schedule for us is this: You learn this week, you take over next week with me still here. Two weeks from now, you have the desk by yourself. So, make sure you ask questions because I won't be here and you don't want to keep calling Police Three to find the answer to a question you should already know."

"I see there is a shotgun and an M16 mounted underneath the desk here. Are they loaded?"

"Well, they would be worthless to you if they weren't loaded. The M16 has a full clip in it, no round in the chamber, and is on safe. The shotgun has five rounds in it with a round in the chamber with the safety on. If you ever have to grab either one, the shit has hit the fan."

"What about chow?"

"We get to enjoy a box lunch! How's that sound?"

"You're kidding, right?"

"Nope, 'fraid not. One of the patrol cars that go to the chow hall around 0200 to eat will bring back a box lunch for you. It will contain a sandwich, fruit, cookies, and juice. In order to relieve you to go yourself, the flight commander would have to take your place. That takes him off the road and unable to respond to any incident that occurs. Once I'm gone, you will be the only desk sergeant trained on this flight. It's not as bad as it sounds, believe me. On a really slow night, you might get to go, but don't count on it."

"What about day shift?"

"You'll get to go to the chow hall a little more often because this place is crawling with everyone during the day. It's much easier to get relief for half an hour when all personnel are here in the building."

"Any other major items to discuss?"

"Yep, one more. Down in the basement, which is through the doorway there, is the cell block, which contains any prisoners that are in our custody. They have to be checked on every two hours by you, and Police Three will come in to let you do that. They have to be escorted in handcuffs to eat at the chow hall, and watched when they shower. If you get a new prisoner in while you are on desk, they have to be processed by two of the men on duty. This includes a strip search and seizure of all items of a personal nature including belts, shoestrings, or anything else that could be used to hang themselves. Now the good news is that they are installing cameras down there so you won't have to keep going down to check on them. The monitor will be placed here at the desk. And for God's sake, if the building has to be evacuated because of fire or some other reason, don't forget any prisoners below."

The phone rang and he answered it with his rank and name. It was an airman calling from one of the maintenance barracks complaining of a fight in progress. He hung up before Lemoyne could get his name.

"Police control to Police Four and Five, report of a fight on the second floor of barracks two twenty-nine. The caller hung up before I could get any further information."

"Police Four and Five, ten-four."

He then moved over to the keyboard and typed in the time and details of the call and who was dispatched to handle it. As it turned out, the fight had broken up by the time the police units arrived. No one knew anything, and the call was cleared.

"You will from time to time get calls from on-base married housing of domestic fights, and the normal stuff that the city police get. We have over four hundred enlisted and officer housing units on base, which does not include the big houses over by the flagpole that house the high-ranking officers."

"Yeah, I made sure I knew the location of all of the commanders on Officers' Row before I left patrol."

"I hope so, because if you ever get a call for police assistance from one of those guys, you better know exactly who it is and where they are. The patrol units know the locations, but your caller might ask you a question about something to do with their neighborhood and you need to know it. When we have high-ranking VIPs, there is a large house three doors down from the base commander that is used to house them."

"Do we get those types often?"

"I would say maybe every six to eight weeks, someone will come in that qualifies for that house; it is usually high-ranking generals or politicians. Speaking of which, on day shift, when they land at the military airport, they are escorted back here to base by a patrol unit. When nukes are landed out there that have to come here to base, more than one patrol unit and all security units are provided as escort and it is a code-three escort. Wherever that nuke is, that area becomes a national security site. We supersede civilian police and everything."

"How often does that happen?"

"Maybe every three months. It's mainly when they change out warheads on the missiles; some come in and some go out. But you'll be on night shift for a while, so that will come in time to you."

"Anything else?"

"That's all I can think of now. So, just sit here and watch and ask questions if something happens or something I do doesn't make sense to you."

THE rest of the night passed quietly as I read the SOPs for the desk. Before I knew it, the sun was coming up, and the day shift was having guard mount and we were relieved. I was tired since my sleep was off with the change back to mid-nights. I got rid of my weapon at the armory, said good night to Todd who was also tired, and headed to the barracks where I hoped my new roommate would be quiet as a mouse. Before I could arrive at my room, however, I felt my stomach growl, and headed to the chow hall for a decent breakfast. After eating, I hit the sack and was glad to see no sign of my roommate.

THE next two weeks went by quickly as I learned everything I could from Sergeant Lemoyne while he was still around. I had been with

Todd four times and on the last occasion of dinner and after-dinner gymnastics, Todd asked me to move in with him. All I would have to do is contribute to the utilities since I wasn't making that much money yet. I was in favor of moving as we would both be working the same shift, and I could get much better sleep than in the barracks. The added benefits were, of course, sex on demand, a more relaxed social life, and a chance to build a relationship with Todd.

In the short time I had gotten to know Todd, I had found a genuinely warm guy underneath a certain amount of macho bullshit, which many men feel compelled to portray to the world. Sexually, I had gotten to the point that I could get him to melt into the mattress with my attentions in bed. I had learned to deftly handle his equipment and bring him a joy that he had never had before. He always complimented me on my efforts in bed.

We decided that when we were on base together, we would eat on base. Otherwise, we would eat at "home." I contributed some money to the food budget, but not as much as I would have liked to contribute. The night before we were to return to duty and I was to take over the desk by myself, I received the required permission from the CO to move off base. It felt good to leave the dully painted and noisy barracks for a house and domestic life.

We ate dinner around 0100 hours, watched television for a couple of hours, and then made mad passionate love on the floor of the living room. By the time we were finished, it was almost 0600 hours, and we went to bed to sleep.

We woke up at 1600 hours feeling well-rested, and decided to watch the news during breakfast. CNN was once again reporting that the Soviets were pushing into the Western Hemisphere in an attempt to force the United States to give them the Balkans. Once again, they were sending Soviet ships to Cuba, although this time, there were no missiles on board as there had been during the Kennedy administration.

Washington was trying to contain the Soviets without force but their efforts were meeting with only limited success.

A central demand of the Soviets was that they wanted us out of the Baltic region, and in turn they would stay out of the Western Hemisphere. Everyone knew that it was their intention to restore the entire old Soviet Union. The new Soviet Union was flush with petrodollars with which to rebuild their rusted military. The only problem with the plan was that some of the Baltic democracies were now members of NATO, which was not about to allow that to happen.

CNN was also reporting that the former KGB had been reactivated and was found to be active in Western countries. Diplomatic protests were coming in from England, France, and Germany, condemning KGB activities within their borders including assassinations of former citizens of Russia who were cooperating with the West. Reportedly, the CIA was stepping up action in conjunction with counter-espionage elements of the FBI in an effort to thwart such conduct within the United States. No one had any real hope that this would be any more successful than it had been during the cold war.

All military bases around the world were told to step up security in an effort to frustrate any infiltration activities by the KGB and their Middle East allies. China was eerily silent during all of this and tried to behave as if this was none of their concern. The fact that the United States owed China more than five hundred billion dollars in loans was a major factor for them being very involved with the crisis. Their pretention of not being interested was being bought by no one.

Todd turned off the television and gave me a worried look. "You do know that if we go to Def Con One, that means war and also means nuclear launch is imminent, right? You will, after all, be one of the first ones notified of a change in defense condition, being on the desk. If that happens, don't plan on ever leaving the desk as we'll be on full action alert and no time off. 'Course, if we launch our missiles, the end of the world is upon us and it really doesn't matter anymore. So, I suggest, Bryce, you learn all you can about your duties, since you might not have a chance to pull any books down if that happens. It will unfold very fast and you won't have much time to think."

"Well, those are happy thoughts to have on my first night as desk sergeant. I suppose there will be at least one Soviet missile coming directly at the base police desk if that happens, huh?"

"I wouldn't be surprised," he answered with a laugh to break the tension.

Chapter 5

AFTER guard mount, I took over the desk solo for my first time. Todd was Police Four, and I had a Police Five along with the flight commander, Sergeant Gray, in Police Three. Gray had been in the Air Force for more than twenty years, and he showed no signs of getting out. The Air Force was his life and he lived for his job and family.

"You ready to take over, Callahan?"

"You bet, Sergeant Gray. My only problem is I don't have a rookie to make the coffee, so I'll have to do it!" I said with a laugh.

"Yeah, well, make it good. As you know, I drink this stuff all night too. If you need me, call me on the radio."

With that I was left alone in the base police building as total silence descended upon me. There were no prisoners in the cells so I didn't have to worry about that. I began my shift report with who was assigned to which police unit, and then brought down the SOP books to begin reading once again the procedures that I might have to implement for various incidents. The night dragged on slowly as no telephone calls came in and everything was routine.

Police Four relieved one of the gate guards so he could eat and then headed to the chow hall himself, where he picked up my box lunch for the night. Instead of eating hot food, he got two box lunches and brought them back to the desk where he ate his with me. When he finished, he went back on the road. Sergeant Gray checked in about every hour or so, and the night finally ended with the rising sun.

The last thing I had to do was finish off my report, sign it, and disburse the copies once Sergeant Gray checked it over. Todd and I headed to the armory, got rid of our weapons, and left base to go home. Once there, we had a light snack and went to bed after about an hour. For my first night, I was glad it had been deadly quiet.

We slept late the next day, catching up on lost sleep over the break. We got up just past 1800 hours and had breakfast. I cooked scrambled eggs, bacon, and toast, and Todd made the coffee. It was exactly what I needed.

"Why don't we watch the news before getting showers?" Todd asked.

"Sure. Let's see what the Soviets are up to today."

We turned on CNN and caught the middle of a story that was being relayed in baited breath by the anchor. The news bulletin was regarding two Soviet subs that had been located off the Atlantic seaboard of the United States. U.S. naval units were now shadowing the subs in an attempt to force them to leave the area. They had not entered the three-mile limit, so there wasn't much the Navy could do.

The camera switched to a news conference at the Pentagon with Chairman of the Joint Chiefs of Staff General McCarty. "We have been in contact with our counterparts in the new Soviet Union in an attempt to ascertain the reasons behind this provocative move on their part. Surely, they must realize that finding two of their subs off our coast was not going to be well-received by us. I'm sorry to report that their only response to our contact was that they could go anywhere in the world they wished to as long as they stayed in international waters."

"Todd, is it me, or are they trying to start a war, a real war, this time?"

"Not sure. But if they are, they're doing all the right things to make it happen. Maybe they think we won't use our nukes."

"God, I hope we don't use our nukes. As we said before, it would end life as we know it. What the hell is wrong with the Soviets?"

"They're playing balls-to-the-wall politics with a loaded gun. They want us out of the Balkans and they want to reabsorb those countries back into the union. It looks like they might be willing to risk war with us to accomplish that goal."

The phone rang and Todd answered it. When he hung up, he looked over at me with a frown on his face. "We've just been recalled to base. It can only mean that we've gone to Def Con Two. Let's move it. Uniform of the day is combat fatigues."

Even though I felt a little stunned, I got up and ran to the bedroom. Todd was stripping off his clothes to get into the shower and told me to do the same. "We need to shower at the same time so we can get back to base within thirty minutes."

I did as he said and we were both washed and rinsed off in under three minutes. We quickly dried each other off, tore into the bedroom and put on our green combat fatigues and combat boots. We were dressed and out the door in just less than twenty minutes from receiving the recall order.

As we rushed to base, my stomach began to tighten up. It failed to ease any when we arrived at the main gate and found the gate guards checking everyone's ID before they were permitted to enter. "Yep, that confirms it. We *are* at Def Con Two; we have a controlled-entry situation on base."

I didn't reply. I just dug out my wallet and showed it to the guys manning the gate. We drove to the armory and drew our side arms. Thirty-two minutes from receiving the call, Todd and I walked into base police headquarters, in uniform and armed. The place was a madhouse, and conversation confirmed our defense condition. Sergeant Gray entered and called our flight together to brief us. I was to take over the desk at once so that the other man on the desk could go get some sleep as he would be working long hours as well. We would have seven police units on the road in addition to the security units. After another twenty minutes, the building was cleared of all personnel but me, and I took over the desk.

I began my report and noted that I was coming on duty three-and-a-half hours earlier than usual as a result of the recall order. Police Three ordered two cars to the main gate to assist in processing the rush of inbound traffic due to the recall. Once everyone got on base, it would return to normal, and the patrols would go mobile once more. That would still leave two extra men on duty at that location until command evaluated manpower needs.

The phone rang and I answered it. It was the Security Police barracks notifying me that rooms had been made up for men who were called in from off base. It was the same guy who had checked me in on my first day. I asked him to save a room for me and Todd, and he assigned room 343 to us.

I radioed Police Three and relayed the barracks information. I would tell Todd later that I had secured us a room. I pulled down the SOP book and looked up "Def Con Two," reading through the list of things to do and checking them off against the previous desk sergeant's report to see if anything had not been completed. To my surprise, every requirement had been met and the only thing I had to do was relay any important updates that came in from Wing Command Post, where the operational center for the base was contained. A security policeman was now also standing guard at that location.

We quickly fell into the routine of a heightened alert and everyone did their jobs by the book. I looked up from my reading to find the CO standing in front of the desk.

"Good evening, sir. May I help you?"

"Callahan, can you handle this post under the circumstances?"

"Yes, sir. I'm sure Sergeant Gray would have kept the last desk sergeant on this post if he thought I couldn't."

"Very well, Callahan. I'm putting my trust and faith in your flight commander and you. I'll be doing a post inspection around base to make sure everyone is on their toes. Our luck, the general will be out running around. I'll be on radio if you need me."

With that he took the keys to his personal patrol car and left the building. Having the CO on the air made it all the more imperative that I didn't fuck up. I waited for about five minutes and requested Police Three to call me from the main gate. He needed to know the major was out on the road.

One hour later, Sergeant Gray came to the desk and informed me that he had met with the major. We were now on a twelve-on, twelve-off shift rotation until we went back to Def Con Three. This news would not sit well with the men but there was nothing anyone could do about it. At midnight, Todd was sent in to relieve me for thirty minutes so I could go to the chow hall and get a normal dinner. Gray figured with these kinds of work hours, I needed regular food like everyone else.

The rest of the shift went without incident and we were relieved of duty a little after 0600 hours. We were due back at 1800 hours to begin our first twelve-hour shift. It was like being back in the field.

Todd and I went directly to the Security Police barracks and checked into our room officially. There were towels on our beds along with sheets and pillowcases.

"Make sure the door's locked so we can share a bed, unless you would rather not," he said with a serious look on his face.

"No, I'm more than fine with that. It will be a little cramped, but I can deal with it to have you next to me," I replied as I locked the door and tried to open it to test the lock.

"We need to be up by 1530 hours so that we can go back to the house and get more uniforms and our personal stuff. I'm not sure how long we're going to be here."

"Okay, let's hit the bed then."

We slid into the narrow bed together and turned into each other's arms. Todd stared into my eyes, smiled and kissed me. "Ya know, I'm getting pretty attached to you. I could get used to this real easy."

"Well, we have to remember that eventually we'll both be transferred and then what do we do?"

"There's a gay guy who works in the section that processes overseas orders, and I'm gonna have a talk with him. I knew him at my last base and he ended up here about a month after I got here. I'll see if I can arrange for us to be sent to the same base. How's that?"

My response was nonverbal. I smiled and kissed him. Before long, we were both sound asleep, with me feeling very secure in Todd's arms.

LATER that day, we woke up from a knock on the door. Todd sprung out of bed and messed up the empty cot before he answered the door. It was the guy in charge of quarters that day, telling us it was time to wake up. Todd thanked the sergeant and closed the door.

"Do you want to shower here or at home?" I asked him.

"We might as well shower here and save time instead of squeezing into the shower at home."

"Oh, I don't know. That has its advantages too," I said with a smile.

We stripped, wrapped the towels around us, and hit the showers. There were another six guys already in them as everyone was beginning the routine to go on duty on the new schedule. I couldn't help but look around at the young guys in all their naked glory. Todd caught my wandering eye, punched me lightly on the shoulder, and shot me a glare that said "Knock it off."

We got back into our uniforms and drove off base. At home we packed a duffel bag with extra uniforms, underwear, and civilian clothes in case we wanted to take a quick walk around without being in uniform. We threw the stuff, which included an alarm clock, into the car and, wasting no time, drove back onto base. When we got back to the barracks, we noticed many of the guys were back in the dayroom watching the television. We figured the news couldn't be good.

We pushed our way into the room and listened. We were right; it wasn't good. The Soviets had just signed an agreement to sell Hugo Chávez of Venezuela two nuclear bombs so that they could protect themselves from "Yankee imperialists."

Chávez was talking to reporters in Caracas, stating that he had the right to buy any weapons system that he wanted to protect the people of his great nation. With the petrodollars Venezuela had, they could buy anything that was for sale.

As expected, the reaction by the United States as well as Venezuela's neighbors was swift and negative. Colombia lodged protests of the sale with anyone who would listen and hinted that this could lead to a war in South America. No one trusted Chávez with a nuke, let alone two of them. The president was to address the nation in one hour.

"Let's get ready for duty and then catch the address before reporting. We should have just enough time to grab some breakfast at the chow hall beforehand."

"Sounds good to me," I replied.

It was starting to dawn on everyone that war was now a real possibility since it was obvious that was what the Soviets appeared to want. They were looking for an excuse to start hostilities that could only end badly for the entire world. There were many members of Congress who wanted a "hands-off" approach to the Soviets as long as they did nothing directly against the United States. They even echoed Chávez, saying that he had a right to buy weapons. The fact that the Soviets had trashed the nuclear non-proliferation treaty didn't appear to matter to them. The other side of the political coin began to call them the "Chamberlains" of the twenty-first century. Appeasement was becoming a dirty word once again in the language of politicians.

Right in the middle of all this were the American people and its military. I had a feeling that our stay in the barracks was not going to be brief. The room grew quiet when the seal of the President of the United States appeared on screen. After a few seconds, the face of President Windsor appeared from the Oval Office.

"My fellow Americans, I come to you this afternoon with the troubling details of what has transpired in recent days between the Soviets and the rest of the world. With the news today that the Soviets have agreed to sell two nuclear weapons to Venezuela, thus introducing these weapons for the first time in the Western Hemisphere outside the United States, a dangerous and volatile situation is now upon us. I have contacted the leadership of the Soviet Union as well as President Chávez, and have requested that this sale be canceled in the interests of peace. Unfortunately, Chávez has maintained his position that he has the right to buy whatever he feels he needs to protect his country. It must be noted that under no circumstances does Venezuela need nuclear weapons to accomplish that task.

"The Soviets, on their part, maintain that they have the right to sell weapons to their allies just as the United States sells weapons to its allies. When I pointed out that we do not sell nuclear weapons to anyone, they responded that it was us who armed the Israelis with nuclear weapons. I categorically deny that the United States has ever played a role in selling nuclear weapons to Israel. In fact, we don't know for sure that they possess nuclear weapons.

"The response of the parties involved in this dangerous situation indicates that they will not heed the request of this government to call off the sale. Therefore, I am calling for an urgent meeting of the U.N. Security Council and will present a case for revoking the membership of the Soviets in that world body. They have chosen to live outside the rules of common sense when it comes to the most destructive force known to mankind. If the resolution passes, we will then request immediate sanctions be initiated again the Soviets in order to encourage them to cease sales of this kind in the future in addition to canceling this sale to Venezuela. Under no circumstances can the United States allow the introduction of nuclear weapons into South America. It should be noted that we have the full support of every nation in South America for our position. The neighbors of Venezuela are unanimous in their position that they do not want nuclear weapons in their backyard under any circumstances.

"I also took the opportunity to lodge a protest with the Soviets regarding their submarines traveling along the east coast of the United States. This protest was met with a declaration of maritime rights to sail anywhere they wish in international waters.

"In closing, I wish to assure the American people that everything that can be done is being done to protect the security of our great nation. I have even offered to meet with the Soviet leadership to work out the problems that now exist between our two governments. They have taken my offer under advisement."

The president ended his brief statement to the nation and the scene switched from the Oval Office to the CNN desk, where analysis of the president's statement began. Todd nudged me and we left the barracks to eat a decent breakfast before reporting for duty.

When we arrived for guard mount, we were informed by Sergeant Gray that all domestic military bases had been notified that unknown individuals had been seen on video surveillance cameras crossing both the Canadian and Mexican borders into the United States. These individuals chose places along the 3,000-mile-long borders that had no official border-patrol presence. From the videos, it appeared that more than 120 men had entered the United States illegally. This constituted a new threat to the security of all military and non-military government sites. We were ordered to increase ground surveillance of all missile sites.

The flight was dismissed to begin the twelve-hour shift and I relieved the day-shift desk sergeant. Other than the almost constant presence of high-ranking officers, nothing new was passed on to me beyond the new orders disclosed at guard mount.

I made fresh coffee before the day sergeant left, and settled in for a long night. After preparing the initial entries for my report, I sat back and began to once again review the procedures I'd have to implement in case of various scenarios.

Several reports of domestic disturbances began to come in around 2300 hours and I dispatched patrols to handle the calls. I had been told in my initial training that these types of calls were rare on base, and here I had received three in the space of an hour. The increased tensions in the world created a harder work environment for the military families on base, and it was beginning to show. Fortunately, no actual violence had occurred in any of the homes that we were called out to. If violence had taken place, the offending party would have been arrested and incarcerated for the night until the base commander could deal with it the next day.

The line from the Wing Command Post lit up and I quickly answered it. I was informed by the duty officer that the commanding general was not at his house, and that he had decided to pull a surprise inspection of our security arrangements around base. I notified Sergeant Gray via radio and took a quick look around the desk area to make sure everything was in order. One place he was bound to inspect was my duty station.

One of the patrol units stopped in to use the restroom and as he was leaving, I heard him yell, "Atten-hut!"

I quickly came to attention as the general strode on in.

"Good evening, airmen. Everything in order?"

"Yes, sir. Everything is good."

When he approached the secured door to my space, I hit the button that let him in.

"Is there anything that I can do for you, sir, or anything that you require?"

"No, but I will have a cup of that coffee if I may?"

"Of course, sir. Let me get it for you."

"As you were; I can get my own coffee, but thank you. Don't let me interrupt your duties, airman."

"Yes, sir."

As the general poured his coffee, I made a quick entry in my report that the wing commander was present. He came up and sat down next to me with his coffee, which was unexpected.

"How many men are on duty tonight with base police, not counting the security teams?"

"General, we have seven men on patrol at the moment, with another three on the main gate. The other gates are closed, of course."

"How often are the closed gates checked during the night?"

"Sir, they are on an hourly check routine."

"Hmm, I wonder if we shouldn't have someone posted on those gates?"

"Well, sir, if we were to have a man at each of the other gates, they would be sitting targets for anyone attacking the base. They would be almost surely killed first and we would never know it."

"Why is that, airman?"

"Sir, they would be sitting in a lit glass booth, surrounded for the most part by total darkness. They would not only be easy to kill, but we might not know it until the next patrol swung by to check on them. If the killers timed the patrol rounds, they would know they had about an hour to do whatever it is they're here to do before the dead security policemen would be found."

"You are correct, of course. Put a note in your shift report for the major to get with the base commander and discuss quickly putting up intense lighting at all entrance points to the base. We may still not put a man on those closed gates, but the extra lighting is cheap additional security."

"Yes, sir. Will do."

"Airman, you don't seem to be nervous at all that I'm here. It's not like the wing commander drops in here very often; in fact, I can't remember ever stopping in here at night."

"No, sir. I'm not nervous. I know you are the commanding general for the wing, but we each have our jobs to do and I am well-trained to do my job."

"Outstanding, airman. Carry on. I'm going to make a couple more checks, and then I'll be in my quarters."

"Yes, sir."

As the general left the secure area, I came to attention as he walked past the front of the raised desk area. I noted what time he left in my report and notified Sergeant Gray that he was here and gone. Later, when the sergeant came back to the desk, I informed him about the general's order to put a note in the report about gate lighting.

The rest of the night passed quietly with no more calls for police service coming in.

CHAPTER 6

THE next morning, we found a note on the door telling us to report to the base theater at 1600 hours for a security briefing. Command used the theater for these kinds of meetings as it was the only place big enough for the squadron to assemble indoors in one location.

Todd and I quickly dressed and headed over to find out what was going on. As we arrived, we found most of the squadron already there with the exception of our mid-night shift guys who were just getting up. I noticed the squadron commander present, along with the base commander and the wing commander. Whatever was going on, it had all the top brass in attendance.

Finally, the base commander called for order and introduced the wing commander to those assembled. He strode up to the microphone in combat fatigues, something that none of us had ever seen before. Usually the general was in dress blues or a flight suit.

"Good afternoon, men. Consider this briefing classified and therefore you are prohibited from discussing anything learned here with anyone outside this auditorium. Approximately four-and-a-half hours ago, the Colorado Highway Patrol made a routine traffic stop on Interstate Twenty-five. The trooper who made that stop was shot dead on the side of the road by the occupants of a dark brown van. Since the trooper had radioed in a vehicle description prior to leaving his patrol car, we have limited information on the suspects. When the trooper did not respond to a radio call checking on his welfare, an alert was put out and units were sent to his location. When they arrived, they found the trooper dead. He had been shot eleven times in a pattern that indicated an automatic weapon.

"An intensive manhunt was launched by ground and air for the van and its occupants. Search helicopters spotted the van north of Denver heading in the direction of Cheyenne. Roadblocks were set up and pursuit was made by ground units with air support providing information on the direction of the van.

"When the vehicle blew a tire, the driver lost control and flipped the van. As police officers approached, the occupants opened fire on the police, killing four more officers. The officers returned fire and killed all but one occupant, who was wounded. What makes this a matter of concern for us here at Warren Air Force Base is that the van was loaded with automatic weapons, explosives, and over twenty thousand dollars in cash. There were no markings on the men's clothes, no identification on any of the occupants, and the prisoner refuses to talk.

"The police believe that these six men could well be some of those who crossed the Mexican border illegally and entered the United States. In light of the weapons and explosives in their possession, we can safely assume that they are not here to create good will with the American people."

An aide walked up to the general and whispered something in his ear. "Excuse me, gentlemen. I have a call regarding this incident." The general walked off the stage and all the men began to talk to their neighbors.

"Todd, do you think they were headed here?"

"I don't know. I guess we have to assume that they were coming here or to the missile fields. Either way, it doesn't sound good."

"Okay, as you were. I just got off the phone with federal agents who are attempting to question the surviving suspect. I've been told that when they adjusted his bandages, he blurted out, "Watch it, you stupid cocksucker, that hurts!" Now while that might seem a reasonable response to sudden intense pain, the suspect was speaking in Russian. I understand that FBI and CIA are on scene and have taken over interrogation.

"I will now assume that we were the destination for these men, assuming that they are Russian Special Forces. The only thing we don't know is exactly what their target was. Even before this last piece of information came to us, I had decided to commence patrol of our silos by helicopter. Security teams will be assigned to each of twenty helicopters with an area of responsibility. Any alarm will require two helicopters to respond to that location. This will put a total of eight security policemen on site within ten to fifteen minutes of the alarm. While that is not an instant response, it is far superior to vehicle response. Major Manchuka, your squadron commander will make the assignments. These patrols will be twenty-four hours a day until further notice. All security policemen will now report for duty in combat fatigues only, regardless of whether or not you are assigned to security response duty or base police.

"Gentlemen, we have to assume that there is an attack on the horizon and you men are the first line of defense for this base as well as the missiles. I have complete confidence in your training and your loyalty to this country and to the Air Force. Take care of each other and stay safe. That's all I have for now. Your CO will now take over this briefing."

"Atten-hut!"

The auditorium stood at attention as the general left the stage and went out a back door. Everyone began talking at once and before long the noise volume rose to a level that made any further briefing impossible unless order was called for.

As the major took the stage, the first sergeant yelled at everyone to sit down and shut up. The room came to order quickly.

"Thank you, First Sergeant. Okay, this is how we're gonna do this. Those of you who are assigned to base police will continue those duties unless more men are needed for the field. Base police will, however, be rotated through the helicopters once a month so that you remain familiar with field procedures. We have to remain a very flexible combat force. Men who are on rotation duty for the field will take over the helicopter duty on a regular basis. Your flight sergeants will take care of assigning you to a schedule. Each launch control facility will still need security policemen on site. However, we are going to take care of this a little differently. Each facility will have four men assigned to it for seven days on, three days off. This way, these men will remain on site to provide protection for the facility and the other personnel assigned there. Remember, alarms and routine checks will now be handled by air, so you will not need to leave the facility unless dire circumstances require it. Therefore, make sure the LCF is locked down tight and keep it that way. Any breach of security is to be met with deadly force. Your primary task is to prevent entrance to the underground launch command capsule by hostile forces.

"I'm sure I don't have to say it, but you people need to be on your toes. There is a strong possibility that we are going to get hit somewhere unless the FBI finds every one of these Russians who have crossed into this country. The fact that they are here at all will increase tensions between the United States and the Soviet Union. They have committed an act of war by sending in what amounts to commandos with a mission to sabotage our missile readiness. If they are this serious about attempting to neutralize our ICBM capabilities, then we must assume they are willing to go to war in order to achieve their objectives. This squadron will see to it that they fail in their mission. No greater responsibility has ever fallen to the security police of any Air Force Base before, including Vietnam and Iraq.

"That's all from me. Your flight sergeants will now break you up into your flights and assignments will be made. Good luck and remember your training."

As the major left the stage, Sergeant Gray came over to the men of the mid-night base police shift. "None of this will affect our schedule or duties unless a few are pulled off for helicopter duty, or we are rotated once a month. But it does mandate that we ratchet up our level of alertness to the maximum. Since we have a full flight, I'm gonna put two-man cars out starting tonight. No one but me rides alone. The security units assigned to the base here will take care of the high security area, which leaves the rest of the base to us as usual."

"Any other changes that you are aware of, Sergeant?" I asked.

"No. But I'll talk to the major quickly about putting an M16 in each patrol vehicle, which you will be responsible for nightly. By the time we go on duty in a little over an hour, I will be able to tell you for sure. Get some food, and be on time."

The entire flight decided to hit the chow hall immediately and then get back to the barracks to put on gun belts. Everyone ate quickly and in silence. All of us were digesting the information provided to us in the briefing. No one was stupid enough not to believe that the level of danger had gone up dramatically with the news that Russians were in the van.

After putting on our weapons gear for duty, we headed to the armory, and then to the headquarters for guard mount. At 1755 hours, we began.

"Okay, as authorized by the major, each unit is to return to the armory once you get your vehicles, and check out an M16 and three clips of ammo. You will put one clip in your weapon, chamber a round, and maintain the weapon in the safety mode. In the morning, you will clear that weapon and turn it in along with your sidearm. Any questions?"

"Sergeant, what do we do with it when getting out on a call?" asked one of the men.

"Good question. On routine calls, secure the M16 in the trunk of your vehicle. On any other call that is out of the ordinary, or one where you are checking on a secure site, one man will carry the weapon. An example of a non-routine call would be any alarm that you are dispatched on. During this time of tension, there will be no training exercises. If you are sent on an alarm call, it is either a false alarm, or real. Consider all alarms as real until told otherwise, and act accordingly. Okay. Hit the road and be alert."

Todd patted me on the back when no one was looking and left the station. I took over the desk from the day-shift desk sergeant and began my shift report, noting the addition of automatic weapons in the patrol cars. After Sergeant Gray left the station, I leaned over and retrieved the desk M16 and inspected it. There was a full clip in the weapon, and the safety was on. I made a similar inspection of the shotgun that hung beneath the M16.

As I looked around my work area, I used the eye of a potential hostile force to judge the weaknesses of the location. It was obvious that the window behind me was the ideal place from which to take out the desk sergeant and, as a result, leave the alarm panel unattended. Anyone who was going to hit the base would surely have been able to review some maps of different locations and might know exactly where the base police desk sergeant was located.

I got up, closed the window, and dropped and closed the blinds. It wouldn't stop a bullet, but it would make it harder to hit me on the first shot. At least that way, I might have a chance to defend myself. I turned on the fan for circulation and made a note in the nightly report of this security deficiency.

If I was honest with myself, I would have to admit to being a little nervous sitting at such a key spot that had alarm monitoring duties of all of the important locations on base. On the mid-night shift, I felt slightly isolated since I was the only person in the entire building. Tonight, it seemed overly quiet, and when the wind picked up I could hear every creak and groan in the building. The phone rang and when I answered I found the wing commander on the phone.

"Callahan, this is General Star. Contact security control and tell them I want one of their armed units patrolling what you guys call 'Officers' Row.' If we get hit, more than likely they'll quickly find their way here to take out the top command structure of the wing. I want this security in place until further notice. Any questions?"

"Yes, sir, just one. You want this detail around the clock, or only during the hours of darkness?"

"Let's make it from 1800 hours until 0600 hours, nightly."

"Yes, sir. I'll set that in motion at once."

I notified security control of the general's order and advised Sergeant Gray of this new order as well as noted it in my shift report. It made sense that a commando team would attempt to take out the command structure of the wing in order to disrupt the flow of orders. It began to feel as if the base were under siege.

In spite of the tension, the rest of the night passed without incident. As the sun began its daily climb into the sky, my eyelids grew heavy and I was glad to see my bed in the barracks. Todd went over to breakfast while I went to bed.

After what seemed to me to be only a couple of minutes, I was awoken by Todd getting into bed with me. I snuggled up to his back as he faced out and fell back asleep after hearing him complain, "I'm too tired to even screw!"

THE next day, we began the routine all over again. After showering and while getting dressed, Todd surprised me with a question I didn't anticipate.

"Bryce, do you think we can build a life together? I'm beginning to really care about you and I think you feel the same way about me; or am I mistaken? I know I mentioned that I could probably get us both transferred to the same base next, but I also feel we might make a life together."

As I finished buttoning my shirt, I took a moment to reflect on my response. I looked over to Todd and said, "I know that I have feelings for you and that I enjoy being with you. I really have no interest in seeing anybody else, so I think I would be more than happy to try and go the distance with you. As for your looks and other talents, well, I am more than satisfied with those."

He walked over and put his arms around me and drew me into a deep kiss. As the kiss continued, my body reacted in a way that said I wanted more than just a kiss. Todd noticed and reached down to give my bulge a squeeze and said, "That will have to wait 'til we're off in the morning."

I sighed and finished dressing while thinking about what Todd had asked me. Could this be the guy I would spend my life with? Before we could discuss it any further, a knock on the door interrupted our privacy.

"Okay, orders for all mid-night shift personnel to report to headquarters immediately!" yelled the sergeant in charge of quarters.

Todd and I looked at each other and grabbed the rest of our gear and headed out the door en route to the armory.

When we reported as ordered at base police headquarters, we found a rack of M16s awaiting us. One of the buck sergeants from the armory was in charge of the weapons and, as each man reported, he was issued an M16 with an ammo belt. After everyone had a weapon, we assembled in the guard mount room where we were called to attention. Our squadron commanding officer was present and took the floor.

"Men, we've been alerted by federal authorities and the Pentagon that plans that pertain to a coordinated attack on this installation have been discovered on one of the dead Russians. We now know for sure that we will be attacked. The Soviet Union has denied any knowledge of the presence of their commandos in this country and alleges that we are using this as provocation to commence a war countdown. Local and state police are out in full force with roadblocks set up on all access points to the base. This should help, but we cannot count on this to prevent commandos from reaching us. Off-duty personnel have been confined to the barracks in order to assist us in discovering anyone roaming around that should not be here. Stop all vehicles that are found on our streets and positively identify the driver and passengers if any, and record that information in your patrol logs. You are to order any personnel encountered who are not on duty to go to their living quarters or barracks and remain there until they are supposed to report for duty. All barracks are to be secured and you will make a check of this while on patrol. If someone comes back to the barracks late, they will have to get the duty sergeant for that barracks to let them in. Further, all base gates will have a patrol team stationed at them throughout the night. You will remain in your vehicles rather than stand watch in the gate houses in order to present less of a target. This means you will be alone at Gate Two and the rear gate, Gate Three. You will be required to check in every thirty minutes with your desk sergeant. If you miss a report time, units will be sent to your location to check on you.

"You men are the defense forces for this base and are being supplemented by security patrols from the weapons division. Should you encounter hostile forces, you are to shoot to kill. Any questions?"

No one raised a hand as everyone contemplated what it meant to be a confirmed target for Soviet commandos. When we were dismissed, I told Todd to stay on his toes and headed for the desk. I read the first shift's report of the day and settled in for what was promising to be a very long night filled with angst on the part of many, including myself. Next I looked up the duress code for the day. The code would change at midnight and I had to make sure that I remembered to switch to the new word. The duress code was the same word for all secured locations. It could be slipped into conversation with another to notify that person that they were under duress and unable to exercise free will. The word in effect until midnight was "snowflake." If I heard the duress code, I would send units to that location in response.

As the building emptied out, I began to receive phone calls from various airmen asking questions about the confinement to barracks. I knew this had never occurred before and it was going to take some getting used to on everyone's part.

My relative quiet was shattered at 2120 hours by a piercing noise from the alarm panel indicating that an alarm had been tripped. I looked over at the panel and saw that it was the officers' club cash room. I went into action.

"Police control to all police units, we have a signal five from the officers' club, Police Three and Four respond code three."

As the units acknowledged the call, I picked up my phone and punched the number "1," which connected me with Gate One, the main base gate.

"Airman Wayne," came the response.

"Close the gate; we have an alarm at the O club."

We both hung up and the main gate, which was the only one open at this time, was closed to all traffic either entering or leaving the base. Since there physically was no actual gate to close, the drivers of the first car in the inbound and outbound lanes were ordered to shut off their engines, which created a barrier to those behind them in traffic.

My next call was to the Wing Command Post notifying them of the alarm. As I hung up from that call, the dispatched units arrived on scene at the officers' club and proceeded to implement standard procedures at an alarm site.

Everything remained silent for a couple of minutes until Police Three notified me that the night manager, who was closing the club early, had accidently triggered the alarm. I notified the main gate to release traffic and informed the Command Post that the alarm was false.

As blood pressures returned to normal, I made coffee and had my first of many cups of the night. The alarm did nothing but increase the tension that everyone was feeling. Would we be attacked tonight? Would I be able to perform well and prevent serious damage from being done to the base?

Todd stopped by the desk to bring me a sandwich from the chow hall. Since he'd also brought one for himself, he quickly ate it while I ate mine. We chatted briefly and he was out the door and back on patrol. Sergeant Gray would not have liked to have found him at the desk area, since all patrols were needed on the road.

The night was passing quietly after the false alarm from the officers' club, with patrols checking in regularly and reporting everything normal. I had once again become engrossed in reviewing my procedures for incidents that could occur, when I noticed that the stationary patrol at Gate Three had not checked in for more than forty-five minutes.

"Police control to Gate Three."

"Police control to Gate Three...."

There was no response and I dispatched two patrol units to check on the unit assigned to that post. Since it was just after 0100 hours in the morning, I was hoping that they merely fell asleep. The alternative was not acceptable.

After another three minutes, the first unit arrived at Gate Three and radioed back in a highly agitated voice.

"Police Five to police control. The Gate Three unit has been hit! Both airmen have been shot and the chain is down on the gate! Please advise!"

Before I could answer, Sergeant Gray came over the air with orders.

"Police control, shut down the base, notify command post, and institute hostile action procedures. Also, have the hospital dispatch an ambulance and medics to this location."

"Ten-four, Police Three. All units copy?"

All police and security units acknowledged the situation as I dispatched a police unit to Officers' Row. I punched in the Gate One number and closed the base for a second time that night and advised the guards what was happening. Next I notified the Wing Command Post that the base was apparently under attack and described the situation at Gate Three.

Since security control monitored the base police channel, they dispatched its units to various locations that housed nuclear materials to reinforce security on scene. The Wing Command Post was notifying both the wing commander as well as the base commander, so those calls I didn't have to make. I next dialed the number for the civilian police and advised them of the situation on base and requested that they have any available unit stand by near Gate One in case they were needed on base.

All my duties were immediate in nature and when I finished the pressing actions, all I had to do was sit and wait for the next thing to happen. I reached under the desk and pulled out the M16 and put it on the counter that ran alongside the desk. Todd radioed in and asked if I was secure and I replied that there was no activity at my location.

As the base began to respond to the shootings of the two security policemen, I took a deep breath and tried to calm myself down. Before I could succeed totally, the second alarm of the night rang in at the desk. This time it was the base Plans and Intelligence vault, which was a high-security location. I immediately dispatched two units to that location and made sure that Police Three knew we had an alarm at the vault. After the initial units acknowledged the call, I updated the main gate so that the security police at that location would be even more on guard than they already were.

Sergeant Gray left one unit on scene with the down security policemen at Gate Two and responded to take command of the alarm at the Plans and Intelligence vault. An additional security unit from weapons security advised they were en route as well. That would give me at least four units on scene at a critical alarm site. Contained at that location were all of the codes for every conceivable aspect of the operation of an ICBM missile base. With those codes, a person could access national security sites within the command network. This was a "protect at all cost" location.

After a few moments, the first responding unit arrived on scene and quickly radioed in.

"Police Four to Police control, be advised I have a wounded lieutenant colonel lying on the ground about fifteen feet from the entrance to the building housing the vault. Continue all units in as fast as possible."

"Ten-four, Police Four. Copy responding units?"

Everyone acknowledged Todd's report of a wounded officer. I once again dialed the base hospital and advised them to dispatch an ambulance and more medics or a doctor to the security perimeter being set up around the alarm site. On-scene units would try to extract the victim so that medical attention could be rendered as quickly as possible. Wing Command Post was monitoring the base police channel and, upon hearing that another shooting had happened at that location, made more notifications, including to NORAD and the Pentagon.

I shut off all of the lights in the immediate desk area so that any hostile forces would be forced to enter my area from a lit room and make for a better target. I would be less visible for an easy shot and thus improve my chances of surviving an attack on the desk. All this was going through my mind as I worried about Todd, who I had not heard from again since his original report on scene. I felt better now that he was no longer alone but had all backup available to him.

Sergeant Gray radioed in that he had command of the scene and advised that they were going to attempt access to the building entrance. As I awaited further word from the scene, the phone began to ring off the hook, with everyone from the general and security police commanding officer to worried residents in the married personnel housing area near the target building calling to find out what was going on. Sirens were heard from the ambulance and some responding security units.

I contacted civilian police communication and requested that their units move up to the gate area and assist with sealing off all three gates. Whoever was on base wasn't going to get off base if I could help it.

Suddenly the silence over the radio was shattered by an urgent warning that shots had been fired inside the building and a confirmation that hostiles were attempting to get into the vault area. Our men had returned fire with one being wounded. The sergeant did not say who the wounded airman was and my anxiety level went through the roof, but I maintained control of my emotions. Additional backup was requested by Sergeant Gray and I punched the phone line to the main gate and ordered two airmen to respond to the vault.

I would leave base entrance security in the hands of civilian police if I had to in order to have sufficient firepower where needed. There were still two airmen left at the gate at this time. As I waited for the additional unit to advise that they had arrived on scene, I heard the door to the headquarters area open from the other room. Since I knew that all my units were busy, I knew it wasn't one of them.

I picked up the M16 and pushed the safety lever to the semiautomatic position and aimed toward the one entrance to the desk area that I could clearly see. No one came through into my room immediately and I grew more tense.

I saw a canister of some kind fly through the air into the outside room and explode, releasing thick white smoke. In response I further shifted the fire selector on my weapon onto full-automatic fire and fired a ten-round burst through the wall into the room from where the canister had been tossed. This left me with ten rounds as I had a twenty-round clip in the weapon. I went back onto semiautomatic fire to conserve ammo. There was no response to my firing, but I could not see a thing and the air became thick inside the desk area where I sat. This lack of visibility worked to my advantage as well as to the advantage of the hostile forces. I stayed low to the floor. When I began to have trouble breathing I crawled up to the desk, which was raised, pulled the radio microphone down onto the floor with me and quickly put out a call for help.

"Police control to all units, base police desk under attack. Request any assistance."

I began to cough so hard that I couldn't speak any further on air. I rolled over to the window and smashed the glass out with the butt of my rifle to get some air into the desk area. As I listened, I heard someone attempting to push open the locked door leading into my secured area and responded at once.

I fired three rounds through the door, placing one round high, one medium, and one low. I heard someone cry out and hit the floor. At least a dozen rounds were returned through the door at me and I cringed down lower than I already was in order not to get hit. I reached over and pulled down the shotgun from its place under the desk and then fired the rest of my M16 rounds back through the door.

The shotgun already had a round in the chamber and all I had to do was push the safety button to the off position and it was ready to fire. The smoke began to clear and whoever was left set off a second smoke canister. I had only one choice that I could think of under the circumstances.

I left the now-empty M16 and rolled back over to the window where I pushed out the screen and as fast as I could literally crawled out the window, falling to the ground, where I was able to get some air and begin to act. I ran the twenty feet to the rear entrance to the building where the hostile forces had entered and came in behind them. I heard more rapid firing and figured that the desk was getting pretty chewed up at this point. If I had stayed there, it was very possible I would have already been killed.

Since they were now making so much noise, I was able to enter the building and come up behind them without them hearing me. I had to be very careful, however, since the lights were on in this outer room and now gave the light advantage to the hostiles.

When the firing stopped, I heard two voices speaking in what sounded to me like Russian. I heard them kick open the locked door to gain access to the desk area and that's when I went into action. I crept below the window area of the desk and came up inside the desk area. Both men were on the upper level of the desk area looking out the window. I didn't hesitate. I fired all five rounds of my shotgun into their bodies, which killed them instantly. One fell out the window while the other slid down onto the floor. I threw down the shotgun and drew my M9 pistol and checked one hostile that was down on the floor in front of the desk area. I had hit him with the M16 when I fired through the door. He was dead.

By now the air had cleared out the smoke fairly well. I got back on the radio and reported an end to hostile action at my location. While I was occupied, a full firefight had broken out within the building housing the vault. Two security policemen were killed in action and all hostiles were killed. My throat tightened up and my heart leapt at the news that we had lost two more men in addition to the two killed at the back gate of the base. Where was Todd?

I requested permission to have the main gate turned over to civilian police with one Air Force security police officer on scene and in charge. Permission was granted.

I next sent a security unit to reinforce the Wing Command Post guard detail as this was also now a viable target if there were any more hostiles still alive on base. Finally, I heard Todd's voice on the radio and experienced a feeling more intense than an orgasm upon realizing that he was not only alive, but apparently unhurt. My eyes clouded up with tears of joy at this realization that the man I now knew I was in love with was coming home at the end of the shift.

Sergeant Gray ran into the building, looking around as he came up to me. He took the tears in my eyes for a reaction to the smoke. As he looked around at the desk, I followed his eyes and became aware of just how much action my duty station had seen. The base police desk sergeant's area was eviscerated by gunfire and blunt force.

"Holy shit, Callahan! How did you survive this and manage to kill the attackers while you were at it?"

"Pure dumb luck, Sergeant Gray. Pure dumb luck."

"Yeah, well, I don't believe that. You had to have kept your wits about you to get through this much destruction. Okay, for now, there isn't much you can do here because literally everything important is destroyed. The alarm panel is all shot to hell, the phones are shot to hell, and the area is no longer secure. I'm transferring dispatch duties to Security Control. For now, remove all papers and manuals from this area and put them in the duty sergeant's office. Continue your report as best you can. Remember also, we aren't sure if there are anymore hostiles on base."

"How many have been killed tonight?"

"Well, you took out three here; we took out four at the vault. So that's seven. Bring your report up to date as best you can, and then take out a patrol car and make a check on Gates Two and Three to make sure the civilian cops are still there. Then, drive through Officers' Row and check on the unit that you sent there to stand watch. Oh, and before you go on the road, secure these weapons that you used."

"Will do, Sergeant."

Chapter 7

By the time the sun came up once again, peace had fallen on the base. The true extent of the carnage could now be seen by all as what had been hidden by darkness now was exposed to the light of day.

Bodies had been removed and consigned to the base morgue; injured security policemen had been treated and released or hospitalized, and new orders were being given as a result of the attack on the base. It was a costly night; four airmen had lost their lives.

No other commandos could be located on base and so it was assumed that all who had entered the base had been killed by the security police. Even the World War II cemetery was searched by Police K-9 units and cleared. Base maintenance personnel were assigned by the dozens to repair the damage at the base police headquarters as well as the Plans and Intelligence vault area. Work was estimated to take up to a week or more to have all affected systems back to normal including the base alarm panel.

Almost everywhere you looked, you could see high-ranking officers inspecting different areas of the base, checking for damage or sabotage. We were finally relieved of duty after a debriefing by the squadron CO, and we headed to the barracks to go to bed. Everyone was exhausted and some were suffering emotional trauma from having lost close friends during the attack.

Todd and I took a quick shower along with about twenty other men and returned to our room. We sat on the lower bunk in stunned silence, reliving everything that had occurred within the past eight hours. We were numb from bursts of adrenaline that eventually wore off, only to be injected with new adrenaline bursts at the next incident.

Finally, I put my arm around Todd and suggested that we get some sleep. Without a word, we climbed into the bunk and got underneath the top sheet with Todd pulling me onto his chest so that my head rested there with my arm over him. I kissed his chest and whispered to him.

"I am so thankful that you came through all that unharmed. At one point I was almost sure that you had been at least wounded at the firefight at the vault."

"Me? What about you? At least I had backup; you were all alone and took on and killed three fucking Russian commandos! If you're not put in for a medal, I'll be surprised."

"Well, the important thing is not medals but the fact that we are alive and in perfect health. The same thing cannot be said for four of our fellow cops. I'm saying a prayer of thanksgiving before I go to sleep."

IN spite of the tension that was easing from our bodies and the emotional night, we both finally fell asleep and slept soundly for eight hours. We were awakened once again by a pounding on the door from the sergeant in charge of quarters.

"Callahan, Claymore! Are you guys in there? Wake up!"

Todd jumped out of bed and messed up his bed to make it appear that he had slept in it and opened the door wearing just his boxer shorts. "Yeah, what is it now?"

"Both of you are to report to the helicopter pad at 1800 hours after you draw your handguns as well as M16s. Additionally, pack uniforms and anything else you will need for a four-day stay in the field. Understand?"

"Yeah, I understand."

Todd closed the door and turned around. "For shit's sake, it looks like we're going flying tonight and we won't be back for almost a week."

I looked over at the clock and saw that it was a little after 1630 hours. We had just ninety minutes to do everything we had to do and report for duty. Since we both showered before we went to bed, we just hit the sinks to shave and brush our teeth. Once that was done, we put on clean combat fatigues and web belts for our sidearms and M16 ammo, and headed to the armory with our duffel bags.

We were issued three ammo magazines and a small box of loose ammo for both our M9s as well as an additional sixty rounds for the M16. We next hit the chow hall as we were both famished, and had a good meal while trying to figure out what was going to be our assignment. We knew it would not be the daily helicopter patrols as we were not coming back for four days. Our guess was that we were merely being flown out to one of the launch facilities so that we could get there quicker.

We caught a lift from one of the security patrols and arrived at the helicopter pad at 1750 hours. Sergeant Gray and the major were both there waiting on our arrival along with four other policemen from the security side of the house.

"Callahan and Claymore, you've got a new duty assignment for at least the next four days. Since the desk area is essentially out of operation for at least a week, you both are being sent into the field for security patrols. Unlike before, this pilot and this chopper will belong to your team. It will land and stay at the same facility as you and the other cops. You will respond by air to any alarm received from any silo within a fifty-mile radius of your location. No trucks this time; we need fast response to anything that comes from those launch sites. Your orders are the same as always: The launch sites are designated deadly force zones and you are authorized to shoot to kill anyone found within the fence line. Any questions?" the major asked.

"Yes, sir. Will there be any other security men on duty there?"

"Yes. The other team you see here is going with you. There will be a total of six men responding to incidents in the field."

"Sir, there aren't enough bunks for that many men."

"We know. You will find a camper on site and two of you will sleep in that. I'm sorry it isn't what you are used to, but lowest ranking will have the camper and on this trip that's you two."

"Yes, sir," Todd responded.

I spoke up, asking what I thought was an obvious question. "Sir, are there any further reports from the FBI about the missiles being targeted?"

"There is nothing precise in this regard. However, the feeling is that there were at least fifteen commandos headed this way and, as you know, we killed seven. That leaves eight unaccounted for, and we must assume that they may try to gain access to our warheads and attempt to detonate them somehow."

"Thank you, sir."

"Okay, men. If there is nothing else, get going and stay on your toes."

We all saluted and headed for the chopper that was just starting up its blade rotation. We were assisted into the cabin of the chopper by ground crew and the door was closed. There were six seats in the passenger compartment, three facing three that sat behind the pilots. The chopper was a UH-1N Huey and was designed for just the type of mission we were on.

The chopper took off into the setting sun, heading to the launch control facility known as Bravo Sierra LCF. As we raced across the sky, I was in awe at the beauty of the landscape as we swiftly passed over it. It was quite clear when we left the urban area and headed out into the plains of Wyoming. After only a twenty-five-minute flight, we came into our landing zone at Bravo Sierra and climbed out, ducking as we ran from the chopper into the LCF. The pilot would shut down the rotors and secure the chopper without us present.

There was now almost no daylight left and dusk was settling in over the area. We received a briefing by the NCO in charge of the LCF, which included the assignment of Todd and me to the camper that was parked outside the building. All sites had been checked on the previous shift and therefore we had nothing to do unless an alarm was activated on one of the sites. We took time while we had it to quickly shower and dress once again since we would be in very close quarters in the back of the camper. We would also keep our weapons with us since we would be outside of the LCF. Since any response required a full component, we were essentially on call duty twenty-four hours a day. The pilot was also on the same schedule as the rest of us, so he slept when he could. If we had an alarm in the middle of the night, he would be required to get up and fly the chopper.

We settled in for the evening to watch television and drink sodas. Unless there was an alarm, we had nothing to do until routine checks the next day. One by one, the other men began to drift off and hit their bunks, leaving only Todd and I watching television. As I looked over at Todd, he smiled at me with a twinkle in his eye, which told me what was on his mind.

"Bryce, wanna go ahead and try and get some sleep now so that we will be ready in the morning for site checks?"

"Sure. Let's take a soda with us and a wet washcloth so we can clean any messes in the back of the camper. No telling how long it's been since it was cleaned real good," I replied with a smile that said yes to his intent.

As we climbed into the back of the camper, we laid our M16's down alongside each of us so they were both out of the way, but easily obtainable for immediate use. We checked the camper over and found everything fairly clean, with fresh sheets for the thin mattresses on the floor of the camper. Since we were not actually on a site, which is what the campers were usually utilized for, we removed our uniforms and neatly folded them and put them into the front seat.

Normally, when an alarm system goes down on site and has to be repaired, a security team is assigned to stay on site until the alarm is restored. The campers were an essential part of that on-site requirement. The Air Force did not expect us to sit up in a truck all night long. One man was to remain on duty in the front while the other got some sleep. Then they would switch halfway through the night.

We had the luxury of both being able to sleep, or to occupy ourselves in other ways in complete privacy, with very little chance of being disturbed unless we had to go on duty. As we lay down on the floor of the camper, Todd took me in his arms and kissed me deeply with tenderness. He practically sucked the air out of my lungs and I melted completely into his arms. When he broke the kiss he looked at me and said, "I wanna make love to you all night if we can."

I smiled at him and replied, "Sounds good to me, but we'll have to control any noise completely in case one of the guys can't sleep and takes a walk around the grounds."

He kicked off his shorts and pushed mine down and off with his foot. As we lay there in the moonlight, I could see his immense dick begin to harden in preparation for action. I bent my head down and first kissed and then nibbled on one of his nipples, which elicited an immediate response from his dick. It became fully erect. I reached down and grabbed it and jerked it up and down while Todd stuck his tongue into my ear and licked each crevice thoroughly, sending chills down my spine. Next he traveled down onto my neck, plastering me with little kisses, being careful not to leave any marks.

As I moaned softly, Todd continued on down my body until he took my dick into his mouth and began to suck gently. As he sucked, I ran my hands over his back and down onto his ass, massaging each cheek. I felt a climax beginning to build already and so I tapped him on the head and he stopped. We then kissed more deeply than I thought was possible as he covered me fully with his body, pinning me against the floor of the camper.

"I love you, Bryce. You know that, right?" Todd asked.

"Yes, and it makes me happy to hear you say it. I love you as well. I was so scared last night for you and even when I was fighting for my own life, all I could wonder was whether or not you were dead. In a way, it drove me to eliminate the attackers as fast as I could. There never was any—"

Before I could finish my sentence, I had a mouth full of tongue once again. He inched his way up my body until he was sitting on my upper chest and I opened my mouth, knowing what he wanted. He began to enter my mouth slowly until he hit the back of my throat and drew in and out. As always, I had difficulty handling his size but was determined to give him the best head I could. As he continued to fuck my mouth, I reached up and tweaked both his nipples, which sent him to a place that he loved. Both became even more erect than they already were. I loved running my hands down over his chest and onto his six-pack abs. How did I get so lucky to find a man like Todd?

As I began to pinch his nipples again, he gave me the signal that he was building to a climax and began to withdraw from my mouth. Instead of allowing that, I pulled back on his hips, keeping him still within me. Todd got the idea and smiled as he began to move back and forth with great urgency, until he covered his mouth to stifle the groan that was now fighting to get out. I felt the rapid splashes of his load fill my mouth and swallowed as fast as I could in order to not get it all over the place.

Finally, when he was finished, he let his now softening dick plop out of my mouth and rolled over onto his back next to me. I grabbed the wet cloth we had brought out and wiped my mouth off as I began to slowly jerk myself off. I enjoyed jerking off while he watched me and, to add to my enjoyment, he began to suck on my right nipple as I jerked faster and faster, until I began to climax. Todd dove down onto my cock and took the load down his throat. After a few moments, he pulled off my dick and rolled back over again with a sigh of contentment.

"Damn, that was good, Bryce. The last few days have been rough and we really haven't felt like sex much. This camper ended up being the perfect answer for us."

"Yeah, but I don't think the Air Force had this in mind when they put the camper here!" I said, and chuckled.

We both pulled on our boxer shorts so all would look normal in case we had visitors. I put my head on his chest and we both fell asleep. As the sun crept up into the sky, one of the other security teams pounded on the back door of the camper. We both sat up with a startled jerk, not knowing what was going on or where we were.

"Come on, guys. Get up, dressed, and eat. It's breakfast time!" shouted Airman Larkin.

"Okay. We'll be there in a few," Todd responded as I began to climb out of the sheets and reach into the front seat for our uniforms.

We got dressed and crawled out of the camper and into the bright sunlight. As we headed toward the building, I looked at Todd and whispered, "That was nice last night. Who would have thought that we would enjoy camping so much?"

Todd responded with a big smile. "Yeah, who woulda thought?"

When we reached the dining room, we each grabbed a plate and went to the chow line. Since we were in this new deployment mode, the base assigned a cook to each LCF so that we didn't have to always eat nuked food. We sat down and began to eat as the LCF master sergeant got up to talk.

"Okay, you guys are going to make your checks today by air, and then return here around noon. The pilot has the landing schedule for which sites are being physically inspected by you guys. You'll go out again this afternoon, and check the rest that you didn't check this morning. When you return this evening, life will be routine with the exception, of course, that you are all on standby for any alarm that might go off during the night. The one exception to this schedule will be a doubling of the guard here at the LCF. This means when you are not in flight, you will rotate with the ground security crew securing this facility. Wing Command wants to be sure that none of the LCFs are taken over. Command is real nervous that all of the suspected Russian commandos have yet to be taken in or killed. Your guard shifts here will be three on and the rest off until your turn comes up in the rotation again. That means that with six of you here, you will only have to pull one guard shift per night. Any questions?"

"Who assigns who to which shift?" asked one of the guys.

"Work it out among yourselves. I shouldn't have to get involved in that. Just make sure your shifts are covered. The man going off duty will be responsible for waking up the man who is replacing him. You don't get off until your replacement is on post."

"Okay, Sarge. We can handle that with no problem."

"Claymore and Callahan, was the camper okay last night, or do you want to rotate with another two guys for the rest of the duty week?"

Todd and I looked at each other and we knew we wanted to stay right where we were. "We'll keep the camper, Sarge. I kinda like sleeping out in the open, although I think I will move the camper to a more concealed location in the compound. Right now, it's a sniper target and that makes sleep a little more difficult."

"Very well. Put it where you like. If you get tired of sleeping in that thing, just let me know."

We finished breakfast and took a quick shower as we had about forty-five minutes before we were scheduled to lift off. It felt good to shave and clean up. The other guys had already done all that before getting dressed so we had the showers to ourselves.

Feeling clean and professional once more, we grabbed a second cup of coffee and downed it before we took off. Then the pilot gave the signal to get ready and after he and his co-pilot checked the aircraft over, they started the engines, the blade began to turn, and we boarded the chopper with our weapons.

We had a total of twenty-three sites to land at, check, and continue on to the next one. The senior sergeant in the group would have to authenticate who we were at each missile site through the means that were available. By the end of the day, we would have checked all forty-six missile sites under our protection. As we took off and gained altitude, we flew away from the sun and toward our first site. I don't know if the pilot was showing off, or just trying to see if any of us would get sick, but he made more than a few sudden banking movements that had us looking at the ground through the side windows. Since we all had radio sets on our heads, we could hear the pilot as well as talk with him.

"Any you boys feeling queasy back there?" the pilot asked.

A couple of the men had changed colors to match our uniforms but I wasn't about to give him the satisfaction of knowing that he was making some of us sick.

"No, sir. We're all just fine here. Is this a training flight for you, lieutenant? Do you have to qualify by showing that you can make sudden turns?" I asked with just a touch of sarcasm in my voice. "I didn't realize that the co-pilot was a flight instructor."

"No, this is not a training flight. Just trying to get us there quickly, that's all," he responded with a note of embarrassment in his voice.

The men all began to chuckle; that is, except for the two who were green. After the brief conversation, the flight smoothed out considerably and the young lieutenant put away the flying circus routine and we flew VFR, or visual flight rules, into our first site. Once a site was spotted, it was simple for the pilot to oversee the area we were entering and then pick a landing site. Flying by this method did not require the instruments that were used at night.

The pilot landed about twenty feet from the side of the site and we bailed out and headed for the entrance gate. Two men began an outside perimeter check of the fence line and the immediate area outside the fence. The rest of us entered the complex after entering the code to access the site. Alarm sensors sent an alarm to both the LCF as well as to Warren Air Force Base alerting those monitoring these alarms that someone had entered the site. Our senior sergeant initiated authentication procedures using a secret code that was only good for one day to verify to the unseen monitors that we were a security team conducting routine checks.

Once that was done, we fanned out and checked the entire inside area of the launch site, looking for anything that did not belong there. We had to ensure that no one threw any bombs onto the site, or tools for use to attempt sabotage. The last thing we did was make sure that there was still a sign posted every twenty-five feet on the fence to announce that this was a shoot-on-site location, so that anyone stupid enough to enter the launch site would know that they could be shot.

We withdrew from the site, secured the entrance gate, and re-boarded the chopper. Once we received a radio signal that all alarms had reset correctly, we took off and repeated the exact same procedures for another twenty-two missile sites. All sites checked secured, and we returned to the LCF for lunch. While there, the chopper was refueled for the afternoon.

The mood was good at lunch as we all were eating freshly prepared food instead of what we were used to getting out in the field. It did make a difference. After relaxing for another twenty minutes, we took off in the chopper once again.

By the end of the day, we were all exhausted from jumping in and out of the chopper more than forty times, running to the sites, and performing fast security sweeps. It was almost 1800 hours when we landed for the day back at the LCF. Once again, we bailed out of the chopper and headed inside while the pilot and co-pilot readied the aircraft for its next flight.

We all washed our hands and faces before sitting down to dinner, eating like it had been days instead of hours since our last meals. Once we were finished, it was time for television and resting up to do it all over again the next day. I found myself wishing I could be alone with Todd, but realized of course that it was impossible. We couldn't very well tell everyone that we were headed to bed before the sun even fully set.

Just after 2130 hours, Todd and I decided to shower and head off to the camper. I was due for guard duty beginning at 0300 hours, and I wanted to sleep before going on duty. Once we got settled into our beds in the camper truck, we talked for a few minutes and Todd held me close.

"Ya know, this duty isn't half-bad when I can sleep with my boyfriend every night," he said with a chuckle. "It was never like this before you came along."

"I'm glad I can make it easier for you to serve your country. I wonder if any of the other guys need this kind of comfort."

That comment got me a tap on the head and an admonition that the only guy I would be comforting was him. It felt good to hear those words. It meant that I was important to Todd and that he did have feelings for me. Could things get any better?

We fell asleep in each other's arms again and were sleeping soundly when we were awoken by a pounding on the camper door.

"Get up. We got an alarm at Bravo-David Four!" yelled the LCF sergeant.

Todd and I quickly got dressed in a bit of a sleep haze and were out of the camper in less than two minutes. Since our weapons were with us in the camper, we were able to board the chopper just as the other security team members were hitting the skids. After buckling in, I bent over to tie my combat boots and flight helmet. I heard the pilot advise us that we were fourteen minutes from touchdown at the alarm.

"Okay, as you remember from today, Bravo-David Four is pretty much isolated in that it is not in a farmer's field or near a town. It is out near the foot of the mountains. The chopper is going to do a flyover of the site first before we land, which will light up any hostiles so that we know to go in hot or not. Now, since it is out in the middle of nowhere, it could just be an animal that has gotten on site and triggered the intrusion alarms. In either case, we'll know shortly," advised the sergeant in charge of the detail.

When the pilot gave us the two-minute warning, the sergeant ordered us all to pull and release the charging handles on our M16s, which chambered the first 5.56-caliber round. All of my training in weapons use flooded back from my memory. The main thing was since it had a rate of fire of 650 to 750 rounds per minute, a twenty-round clip would be gone in a second if you didn't control your fire.

"Get ready. We're here. I'm flying over site in ten seconds," the pilot advised.

The men near the windows were pinned to the Plexiglas looking at the ground as we flew over. Todd, who was sitting to my right, shouted out, "We got movement on site!" This was confirmed by another airman and we knew we had a good alarm.

The pilot radioed in to Warren that we had possible hostiles on location and that we were landing and engaging. With that, the lieutenant set the chopper down about a hundred yards from the launch site and we bailed out faster than we had at any time during the previous day. We broke up into two teams, with one team heading toward the rear of the site, while my team worked our way toward the front of the site. There were no lights on, of course, so it was hard to see exactly what we were getting into.

"We got a vehicle about a hundred and fifty yards behind the site!" shouted out one of the airmen. They broke off their forward motion and headed toward the vehicle while spreading out so that they were not bunched up.

As we drew to within twenty-five yards, shots suddenly rang out, striking the other two members of my small team. Both men went down, howling with pain as I returned fire in the direction of the muzzle flashes that I had seen. I didn't remember my training, and ran through my clip before I could take my finger off the trigger. Instead of reloading, I threw down my weapon and took up one of the rifles from a fallen airman.

The second team also encountered fire from the vehicle, which was met with a determined rate of return fire. As this was going on, the chopper went airborne and reported into base that we had a firefight going on at the launch site. This triggered an alarm called a "covered wagon," that went all the way to the White House via the Pentagon. Anything that happened like this at a missile silo went up the entire National Command Authority chain as a flash message. The immediate threat was that there was gunfire being exchanged with hostile forces over an ICBM missile that carried ten nuclear warheads known as a MIRV and could effectively wipe out a three-state area were it to somehow be activated and triggered. The only true safeguard was that these missiles are not supposed to arm themselves unless in flight.

I regained control of my adrenaline and fired short three-round bursts at two figures lying on the ground inside the missile site. I was lucky enough to be behind a large rock and could take aim in a much safer fashion as I tried to take out the enemy. Finally, I heard one of the hostiles yell out when I put a couple of rounds through his shoulder and took him out of commission. Wounds from an M16 are horrible and most often lead to the death of a combatant even if he is only wounded.

The world seemed to rock as my vision blurred due to the force of an explosion that came from what used to be a van that the other team was firing on. Flames shot up fifty feet into the air, killing all within the vehicle. At the same time, the fire lit up the launch site and I was able to take out the second hostile when he became clearly visible. After parts of the van ceased to rain down on the area, all became quiet except for the sound of the chopper in the sky and the crackle of small fires that were started in the brush from the van explosion.

One member of the other team was also wounded by gunfire, which left only three of us in good condition. While it was hard for the other men to hear as a result of being so close to the explosion, they were able to function. One of them entered the site along with me to check the hostiles and see if they had been able to do anything to the missile site itself. The second man I shot was dead as the round went through his head, taking most of it off his shoulders. The other man was bleeding profusely and I did not expect him to live. We kicked all the weapons away from the men on the ground and I hand-searched the wounded man for other weapons. He began to plead with me in Russian, though of course I had no idea what he was saying. While the second airman stayed with the prisoner, I ran over to the various components of the site looking for problems. I found one. Placed directly on top of the protective cover to the missile was what appeared to me to be a bomb of some kind. The obvious intent was to blow open the missile silo, giving the commandos access to the ICBM.

When I ran back to the prisoner and airman guarding him, the prisoner was dead. I had killed both commandos. The sergeant in charge of the security team entered the site and I informed him of what I had found. He ordered us to vacate the site until instructions were received from base. He radioed up to the chopper what we had found and requested orders.

It was then that I noticed that Todd was absent. I asked the sergeant where he was, afraid of the answer.

"He's lying over there. He's been hit in the left shoulder. Haney is trying to administer first aid to him and the others. We may lose Albertson."

I panicked and ran over to where Todd and Haney were. I knelt down and was relieved to find Todd's eyes open at least. "How bad is it? Are you in a lot of pain?"

"Hell yeah, I'm in pain! I've been shot. What did you expect?" he responded with a slight smile, which told me he was trying not to worry me.

"Okay. We've got to move way back beyond the large boulders over there. There's a bomb on site and if it goes off, I don't want any more men injured or killed. Let's move!" the sergeant shouted.

After a few minutes, everyone was resettled safely behind the boulders. All of the wounded needed immediate medical attention, which was relayed to the chopper. The pilot was doing an aerial check of the immediate vicinity to ensure that there were no other commandos to deal with. With the death of our only prisoner, we had no surviving enemy to guard. It had been an expensive raid, however, with three men wounded, and two almost deaf. Somehow, I was the only one who came out unscathed.

The pilot radioed down to us that he was landing as the area was clear of any other hostiles. The state police had also been notified and were en route, but it would take some time for them to arrive due to our location.

The pilot got out of the chopper and ran over to us. "Two things: The base had another attack tonight while this was going on. They tried to take out General Star at his residence. What they didn't count on was the general carrying around a forty-five caliber automatic. He killed both assailants. Second, a chopper has been dispatched with medical personnel and more security troops. Once they arrive, they will take charge of our wounded and you other three will be flown back to base—not the LCF for medical care and debriefings. ETA for the choppers is about another twenty minutes. Keep pressure on the wounds and watch for signs of shock. Here are two blankets from on board the chopper. Cover them up the best you can."

"What about the bomb? We can't just let it sit where it is!" I asked.

"Well, that was the other thing. They want to know if you feel you can move the bomb off site and into the field?"

"Who, *me*? Are you shitting me, Lieutenant? They want me to move a fucking bomb when I have zero training dealing with bombs other than evacuating the area? Are they crazy?"

"Callahan, they are worried that if it goes off, it will crack the warheads underneath and release radioactive material into the air. There is a major freshwater source, just over those hills, that feeds into the drinking water for this part of the entire state. We can't let it be contaminated."

"Well, they should have thought of that before they put the damn missile here!"

"I'm just passing along the request. They are not ordering you to do this; they are asking you to do it."

"Oh, that makes all the difference in the world then! As long as it's not an order, I'd be happy to try and blow myself up!"

"Callahan, it will take the army at least an hour and a half to get a disposal team out here from the nearest Army post that has a unit. It's up to you."

I got up off the ground, gave the lieutenant a "go fuck yourself," look, and headed back to the launch site. I threw a curse at the dead commandos on the ground that questioned the moral characters of their mothers, and gingerly approached the bomb. I was startled slightly when a shaft of bright light hit me and the bomb and it took me a moment to realize that the pilot had turned on one of his small spotlights and aimed it at me.

From what I could tell, which wasn't much, it appeared to be an electronic bomb, and not one of the old "light the fuse and run like hell" kind. As I knelt down to take a closer look, I saw what appeared to be a cover made of metal with a thumb indentation where you would place a finger to open the cover. I slowly put my hand on the cover and lifted it up, revealing a sight that sent a chill though my entire body and almost made me release the contents of my kidneys all over myself.

Inside the outer case was a timing device that had analog numbers, which were in fact ticking away. The numbers that were clearly visible read 4:21, and were counting down. I yelled that it was going off in about four minutes and to get way back. I had no idea what material was in the bomb and hoped that it did not have movement sensors that would trip the explosive circuit if moved. I really didn't have any time to over-think it.

I closed the cover and picked up the entire device, which was about two feet long and two-and-a-half-feet wide. It weighed about forty pounds and I was able to easily lift it. As I took my first steps toward the gate, my heart raced and my palms began to perspire. Since I was sure now that it wasn't going to be triggered by my carrying it, I moved as quickly as I could without running. I turned once outside the gate and headed away from the missile silo and my friends.

I tried to keep a count in my head of the number of seconds that were ticking away, remembering that I had to give myself enough time to get away from the bomb before it detonated. I walked until I thought I had about ninety seconds left, set the bomb down and ran like hell toward my friends. I never slowed down until I reached them. In my head, I had counted to zero about two seconds before a great explosion rocked the earth. It literally knocked me to the ground. Once again, the sound was deafening and the entire area was lit up by the fire produced by the explosion. Little bits of rock, dirt, and pieces of plant life rained down upon us as we covered our heads. After about thirty seconds, everything grew quiet once more and the area was in darkness except for the spotlight still facing toward where the bomb used to be.

"Well, I guess they meant to blow up the place," observed the pilot dryly. "Good job, Callahan. That took a lot of balls to do and you pulled it off. Little doubt in my mind that had the explosion occurred where the bomb originally was, we would have a badly damaged ICBM leaking radiation all over the place. You'll get a medal for this."

"Right now, I would settle for my bed back on base and a very large scotch."

Two choppers landed by our chopper and discharged medical personnel and additional security teams. They quickly began to work on the wounded and confirmed that the commandos were dead. The new security team was ordered to remain on site with one chopper standing by for them. The rest of us took off in the remaining choppers and headed back to Warren Air Force Base. We had all earned our pay that night.

Chapter 8

AFTER landing at the base hospital landing pad, our wounded were quickly taken into surgery and the rest of us were placed in an exam room where more doctors waited to go over us with tremendous attention to detail. The men who had suffered hearing loss were told it would be only temporary and that by morning, most of their normal hearing would return. I was given a clean bill of health and told to report to the commanding officer immediately. The only thing I wanted to do was to stand by until Todd was out of surgery and I was sure he was going to be okay. The new love of my life had been shot by a Russian commando and I was not amused. There had to be some serious payback for this kind of crap on American soil. One of the doctors said he would call over to base police as soon as Todd and the others came out of surgery with an update on their conditions. That would have to do for me, as orders were orders. Just as I left the hospital, the national colors were being raised on the base flagpole. As required, all movement ceased and all eyes focused on the stars and stripes being raised. Those of us in uniform saluted until the color detail made up of base police dropped their salutes. When the guys saw me, they wanted to know all the details about what had happened and gave me a ride back to the desk so I could report as ordered.

The sun was now up and the base was already alive with activity. Between the attempted assassination of the general and the assault on the missile silo, no one had gotten a full night's sleep. I entered the building that housed the rebuilt base police desk as well as the security police squadron offices. This time when the CO's clerk began to make a wisecrack about the mess my uniform was in, I told him to shut up and tell the major that I was reporting.

"Callahan, is that you out there?" yelled the major.

"Yes, sir."

"Well, get in here."

I walked in and stopped four paces before the major's desk and saluted, saying, "Airman Callahan reporting as ordered, sir."

"Sit down, Callahan. Make yourself comfortable. You've had a rough night from what I understand so far. Tell me in detail what happened at Bravo-David Four."

After I gave a full description of the events in the field, the major leaned back in his chair. As he stared at the ceiling he said, "Last time you were in here, you were here for shooting a snake. I wasn't all that happy. This time, Callahan, you're in my office for shooting snakes again. Only this time, they were Russian snakes!" he said as he looked at me again with a gigantic smile on his face.

"Callahan, I couldn't be more proud of you and the other members of your team. You fulfilled your mission and the fact that you removed a bomb from over an ICBM at great personal risk is the single greatest act of bravery ever engaged in by a member of this command since we were established. By the way, it wasn't my suggestion that you remove the bomb; it was the general's. He'll be wanting to talk to you before you hit the sack. By the way, I'm putting you in for medals for last night's action. In fact, I'm recommending your entire team for a Presidential Unit Citation."

The phone interrupted the major and he took the call. It was the base hospital.

"I see. Very well. Keep me informed," the major said and hung up the phone.

"Well, all of your teammates came out of surgery alive and are predicted to make a full recovery. You're one lucky man to have been the only one not injured or killed in that firefight. Five dead Russians. Amazing. Well, that's all I have for you, Callahan. Change uniforms and report to the general at his office."

"Yes, sir. What uniform should I wear, sir? Combat fatigues or dress blues?" I asked.

"The order for all security policemen to be in fatigues has not been lifted, so report in a fresh set of greens."

"Yes, sir."

I saluted once again and left the office, not even bothering to give the wiseass at the clerk's desk a look. As I was walking down the hall, the chief master sergeant for the squadron stopped me and wanted a full briefing. I didn't like this man at all and I tried to keep from showing it. "Sorry, Sergeant. I've been told to report immediately to the general and then hit the sack."

"Very well, airman. Carry out your orders."

I smiled all the way out of the building and hurried to the barracks. Todd was on my mind the whole time I was changing into a fresh uniform. I was relieved that he had no problems in surgery, but still wanted to know how much damage was done to his shoulder. Was he in pain? Was there anything I could do for him? I decided to visit him before I went to bed for the day.

After reporting to the general, I was told once again to sit down, which was unusual. Normally, you always stood up for a conversation in the general's office, with him being the only one seated. General Star had of course talked with me before when I was on the desk, so we had some background.

He wanted all the details just as the major had wanted. When I finished, he had questions.

"Callahan, you know it was me that requested that you move that bomb and that I had no choice but to ask it, right?"

"Yes, sir; although my immediate reaction surprised the pilot who relayed the request."

"Oh? What was your reaction?"

"Well, sir, begging the general's pardon, but I don't wish to insult you, nor would it be wise for me to insult you."

He laughed out loud. "Hell, Callahan, the bastards tried to shoot me last night in my own damn home! In front of my wife! Whatever you said in response to my request has to pale in comparison to that!"

"Yes, sir, and I'm glad you made it out of that situation all right. Well, sir, I wondered about the sanity of whoever gave me that request, and took a special note that it was a request and not an order. I might have said a couple of other things."

He laughed once again. "Callahan, I've already had a report from the pilot who was there and I got to tell you, son, you are one brave son of a bitch. You're going to get a medal, no doubt, for your actions that went above and beyond the call of duty. You do realize, don't you, how important it was to remove that device from directly on top of the missile, right?"

"Yes, sir, I understand that the explosion could have cracked the warheads and released radioactivity into the atmosphere."

"You're damn right, son, and that would have been the least of it. I had no option but to ask you. What are you doing the rest of the day?"

"Well, sir, my roommate and best friend was wounded in the firefight and is in the base hospital. I'm going to go visit him before I go to bed."

"Tell you what; I'll have my car take you over there so that you don't have to walk. When you're through, call the desk and have a patrol car pick you up and take you to the barracks. I'm giving you tonight off from duty and will notify your commander. I'll be talking to you again, son, and good job once more."

The general stood up, which made me stand up. He shook my hand, and I saluted and left his office. The general shouted to his driver, who was in the outer office, to take me to the hospital.

I had no idea what medal I would be put in for, but it really didn't matter to me all that much. What mattered most was Todd and our future together and whether or not his wound would impact that somehow.

After the driver dropped me off at the hospital, I went in and tried to find Todd's room number. The nurse wouldn't give it to me, saying he should not have any visitors. I was going to argue with her, but it would have done no good and she was a second lieutenant and they just don't like to be challenged. After going down the hallway, I ran into the doctor who had examined me earlier.

"Excuse me, doctor, but the general sent me over here to look in on Sergeant Todd Claymore and make sure he was doing okay. The nurse refused to give me his room number. Should I let the general know that I couldn't see him, or can you tell me where he's at?"

"Normally, the nurse is correct. When someone comes out of surgery for this type of wound, visitors are restricted. But since you're here with the general's interest in hand, I'll show you to his room and let the nurse know you are the exception whenever you want to visit him. No need to bother General Star with this."

I smiled as I followed the doctor. I'd played the situation perfectly without lying about the general's involvement. When the doctor opened the door, I was pleased to see that Todd had a private room rather than a ward bed. Because Todd was a sergeant, he got his own room while airmen had to share a large room with as many as five other men.

"Okay, he is still sleeping from the anesthesia, so try not to wake him. If he does wake up, he will be very groggy. Please don't stay longer than fifteen minutes. Deal?"

"Yes, sir, that's fine. I appreciate your making the exception for my roommate."

When the door closed, I walked up to the bed and looked down on my man. He was heavily bandaged up around his shoulder and with tubes coming out of his arms that were hooked up to IV solutions. I quickly bent over the bed and gave Todd a kiss on his forehead and whispered, "I'm here, baby. You're gonna be all right."

Before I could sit down in the chair next to the bed, a scene from Snow White played out before my eyes. His eyelids flickered and one eye popped open and then the other. My kiss had brought him back to life! I giggled to myself and shoved the cartoon scene out of my head.

"Hi, honey. I'm here. How do you feel?"

Todd turned his head and looked at me, trying to focus. "That's the second time you've asked me that dumb-ass question! I feel like I've been shot!" He started to snort with laughter and then began to cough. His coughing continued for a few seconds and a nurse popped in.

"Sergeant, how do you feel?" asked the innocent nurse.

I began to laugh, which elicited a rude look from the nurse, and I shut up. "Don't know what's so funny about that question, airman!" she admonished.

"Nurse, I feel like I've been shot. That's how I feel!"

I couldn't help myself; I laughed out loud. "Well, obviously there is something I've missed going on here between you two," she said.

"Nurse, it's just that I've asked him that question twice; once last night after he was shot, and moments ago before you came in. His response was the same to me as it was to you with a little extra thrown in."

"I see. Well, thank you for not letting loose with the blue language, Sergeant. Your coughing is a natural reaction after having anesthesia. It's the lungs clearing themselves. It should cease in another hour or so. Other than that, are you... well, are you in pain?" she said catching herself.

"Yes, as a matter of fact, I feel like I've been hit by a truck."

"Well, I'll be back with a shot that will take care of that."

With that the nurse left and I began to chuckle once more. "Coward. Why didn't you say to her what you said to me?"

"'Cause you're not going to be sticking me with needles for the next few days, that's why."

"Chicken. I was awful worried about you, Todd. All I could think about was you while I was with the major and the general this morning."

"You spoke with the general?"

"Yeah. After giving me that order that wasn't an order last night, I guess he felt he owed me an explanation. Ya know, they tried to shoot his ass last night too!"

"Hold on. What order that wasn't an order did he give you last night? Was he on scene?"

"No. His suggestion was relayed to me via the pilot that we carry the bomb off site so it wouldn't blow up the missile. Since I was the only guy not wounded or deaf, I was elected. The pilot damn sure wasn't going to do it. Outside his pay grade...."

"Did it go off?"

"Oh hell yeah, it went off. Made the night into day it was so bright. But the missile was safe."

"You said they tried to shoot the old man?"

"Yeah, two gunmen hit his house while we were handling the firefight. He shot and killed them both. Seems the general carries a forty-five around his house and was armed when they broke in. Shot and killed them both."

"Damn.... The Russians are really crazy. We could go to war over this. You know that, right?"

"Yeah, I figured we might. But if we launch, it's the end of the human race as we know it. There has to be a better way."

The nurse came back in with a needle in her hand. She moved the sheet aside, pulled Todd's PJ bottoms down slightly and stuck it in. He winced in pain, but soon had a very peaceful look on his face as his eyes slowly closed.

"He'll be out for a while now, airman."

"What did you give him?"

"Morphine."

I left with the nurse and called the desk for a ride. I didn't need a shot to go to sleep. I was beat. I didn't take a shower or anything; I just went directly to my room and climbed into bed. I slept for almost eight hours straight. I was awoken by banging on my door from other men in my unit telling me to get ready for work. I yelled back that I had the night off and received a great deal of verbal abuse for my good luck.

I got up, showered, and climbed into a uniform even though I wasn't on duty that night. I intended to hit the chow hall, eat, and then head over to the base hospital to visit Todd again. I still sensed an intense feeling of uneasiness from almost everyone I encountered. The entire base knew about both attacks the night before and on top of the full-out assault we had already fended off, people's nerves were beginning to fray.

The base theater was reopened with security troops posted on guard outside. The base commander wanted airmen to be able to relax and watch a movie but did not want a very inviting target to be accessible should more commandos breach base security.

After eating what turned about to be a really fine meal, I once again headed to the hospital. Now that it was getting dark outside, I found myself looking over my shoulder for anyone suspicious. There was a television on in the chow hall and news of the two attacks was on the evening news. A similar attack had occurred at Minot Air Force Base without success. Two airmen had been killed in the attack, however. The president was addressing a joint session of Congress the day after tomorrow and speculation about what he would say was running rampant.

This time I didn't bother to check in with the nursing station, bypassing any potential trouble from another nurse trying to protect my guy from visitors. I found Todd wide awake and moaning a little bit from the pain. His tray of food sat uneaten on the table next to the bed.

When he saw me walk into the room, his face lit up like a Christmas tree. He was very happy to see me and that made me feel better as well.

"Hi, roomie. Good to see you again. I won't ask you how you feel; I think we've covered that topic enough already," I said with a smile.

"Hey, guy. Good to see you. Were you here earlier today? I seem to recall a visit from you, but if you did come, I don't remember a thing about it."

"Yes, I was here after doing an end run around Nurse Ratchet who didn't want me bothering you. I dropped the general's name with your doctor, and that got me in."

"Well, I'm glad you were persistent even though I don't remember anything about the visit. Shouldn't you be at work by now? You're not armed, so I take it you're not on duty?"

"No, the general gave me the night off as a small reward for surviving the firefight. I'm back on duty tomorrow, though."

I glanced at the door and gave Todd a quick hit-and-run kiss. He smiled and said he wanted a lot more than that. "I thought you were getting better, and now I know it. You're horny again! Always a good sign."

"You make me horny. I can't help it. Why don't you jump in bed here?"

"Sure, that would be a great idea. Since 'don't ask, don't screw' hasn't been repealed yet, I don't think that's a good idea."

"Coward."

"Not according to the general and major. In fact, I'm being put in for some medal, along with the rest of you guys who got wounded."

"Get out. Really?"

"Yep. The bastards also hit Minot up in North Dakota. They failed there too, but took out two security policemen. All of our guys are gonna live. I thought for sure one would die, but you all are going to make it."

"Have you heard anything about what the country is going to do about this? I mean, we've been royally attacked! There has to be a military response."

"The president is going to address Congress on that very issue tomorrow. Frankly, if he declares war on Russia, our lives may be over. This base is surely on the target list to be hit. If you're still in here when that happens, I'm gonna be here with you at the end."

"You promise?"

"Wouldn't have it any other way, my lover."

"Well, let's hope we handle this without going to war. Hell, I've even picked out our next base if we can pull that off."

"Oh? What base?"

"How's Italy sound? Aviano Air Force Base up in the northern part of the country. The Thirty-First Fighter Wing is assigned there and it would be great duty; just be regular old base cops, no nukes, none of this shit. How's it sound?"

"I love Italy. The men are as handsome as the women are beautiful. And the food, oh my God, the food! Hell yeah, I'd go for Italy in a heartbeat. I could take weeks just sightseeing in that country. You realize the history contained within the Italian borders?"

"Okay, I get it! You like the idea of going to Italy together. Okay, well, first I need to heal up from this shoulder wound, and then we have to survive the crazy Russians, and then I can maybe get us transferred to Italy. It wouldn't be for at least a year anyway, but at least we would know where we were going."

"Okay, it's a deal. I'll leave it up to you to handle all that."

"What medal are you being put in for?"

"I have no idea. I wasn't wounded so it won't be the Purple Heart like you. Why? Is that important?"

"Well, it could be. If you get a major medal, it gives you some weight to request a particular duty station for your overseas tour. The Air Force is very unlikely to deny such a request."

"Well, let's not worry about all that just yet. The most important thing is for you to get well, and for the president not to blow up the world tomorrow. So for now, you need to be sleeping and doing what they tell you to do here."

"Well, I do have one cute male nurse who got a look at what I'm packing, and boy did he light up. I suppose I could always get a little action to make me feel better."

"I find out you're doing that, and I'll make sure I'm here the next time you're knocked out on morphine or some such shit, and I'll fix it so your dick never gets hard again!"

"Okay, okay. How 'bout I just pinch him on the ass?"

"That's fine, but anything more and I warned you!"

The nurse came in and told me I would have to leave. It was time for more shots and Todd would be out very soon. I shook hands with him since I couldn't give him a kiss. Leaving the room. I shot him a look over my shoulder and we both smiled at each other as the nurse jammed him again with a needle in the butt.

It was an hour before the next show at the base theater so I headed that way. The cost was only two bucks and the popcorn was cheap. It beat sitting around the barracks wondering if the world was going to end tomorrow. Since I was back on duty the next night, I had to stay up most of tonight so that I could sleep tomorrow. This was the only part I didn't like about night shift.

After the movie, I headed back to the barracks as some of my buddies went by in a patrol car yelling obscenities at me for having the night off. I gave them the finger and continued my walk. Would there be another attack somewhere tonight? Had we finally taken out all of the commandos sent to attack Warren Air Force Base? Well, I would be up all night anyway, but I would be in the dayroom watching television. If another attacked happened, I would report to the armory and draw my weapons and assist where needed.

But there wasn't another attack and the night passed peacefully. At 0500 hours, I headed over to the chow hall, ate a quick breakfast and headed back to try to get some sleep. I would set my alarm for 1400 hours, when the president was scheduled to address Congress. No matter what he had to say, I would visit Todd after that, and then begin my normal routine. I was to report once again to the newly renovated desk sergeant's area. We were still on twelve-hour shifts, so I would have to eat, shower, dress, and report for duty. I had some trouble closing my eyes, wondering what the president was going to say.

CHAPTER 9

AT a little before 1400 hours, I woke up to my alarm, threw on some pants and a T-shirt, and headed down to the dayroom, which was already full of men. I wedged my way into the room and sat down between two of the overstuffed chairs just as the network news broke in on regularly scheduled programming.

"This is a CBS News special report: A Presidential address to a joint session of Congress on the recent military action within the borders of the United States."

The camera focused on the great seal of the Congress. The mumbling that could be heard from the members was suddenly silenced as the House Sergeant at Arms made the announcement: "Madam Speaker! The President of the United States!"

Everyone assembled in the chamber rose and applauded as President Windsor walked down the aisle and shook hands with the Speaker of the House and the President of the Senate, his vice-president. He then turned and faced the audience, who quickly sat down. Everyone knew this was not a normal speech by the president. The room grew quiet as the president prepared to speak.

"Madam Speaker, Vice-President Wilson, members of Congress, distinguished guests, and my fellow Americans: I come before you today with a heavy soul and a profound sense of bewilderment. Over the past seventy-two hours, hostile military action was initiated against the United States by what have been identified as Soviet Commandos who were covertly introduced into the United States across the Mexican border. As many as twenty Soviet commandos attacked Francis E. Warren Air Force Base, twice in two nights, and attempted to sabotage by explosive devices one of our ICBMs, while it rested within its silo. Additionally, Minot Air Force Base in North Dakota was also attacked in an attempt to get to a nuclear weapon. These attacks failed. They failed but at a cost of seven or more airmen who were killed in action defending our national nuclear capabilities. In addition, several more airmen were wounded or injured in action with these hostile forces, along with millions of dollars' worth of damage to Air Force property.

"We had intelligence shortly after these men crossed the border that they had entered the United States, but we were unable to track them and unable to prevent the attacks I have mentioned. They came heavily armed, with plans and maps, and knew what their targets were. Interrogation provided their origin and their purpose.

"When the Soviet Union was asked to explain these attacks, we were told they were rogue commandos and not under the control or direction of the Soviet High Command. We were told that a certain Soviet general by the name of Victor Antonov had gone rogue and was intentionally trying to start a war between the United States and the Soviet Union. We have been told that the Soviet missile base, Pinsk South, is now under the control of General Antonov and his forces. Certain elements of the Soviet Air Force are in league with Antonov, which explains how their commandos were transported around the world to our backyard.

"The big question about this information is, do we believe them? If we do, is the Soviet Air Force able to cut off the command and control functions of the missiles Antonov now controls? How much danger are the United States and its allies in due to this threat?

"We have been told that as best they can tell, a total of twenty-four commandos were introduced into the United States with sufficient supplies for a five-day campaign. If this is accurate information, then we have located all but one commando. He is being hunted as we speak.

"What should our immediate response be to this information from the Soviet Union? How do we protect ourselves from being attacked with nuclear missiles? We have two options open to us. We can demand that the Soviets either retake the Pinsk South missile base or destroy it completely by whatever means necessary. Or, we can launch our own missile targeted to take out that base within a few hours.

"The Soviets have told us that if we take out that base, then a state of war will exist between our two countries that will in all likelihood involve our nuclear forces. As you know, should there be a general exchange of missiles between us and the Soviets, the world will cease to exist as we now know it. It is predicted that within two years from an all-out nuclear war, the planet will begin to die along with the human and animal population of the world. There is absolutely no chance that mankind will survive such a war.

"As for those living underground in shelters and bunkers; yes, they will survive. They will also eventually die when their food, air, or water runs out. They only delay their eventual deaths. This is not a picture that is comfortable for anyone hearing it but it is the reality of the situation we find ourselves in. This is a decision that I refuse to make without consulting Congress.

"Therefore, I ask you here and now for a 'Sense of Congress Resolution," that notifies the Soviet Union they have forty-eight hours in which to take control over the base that is now in rebel hands. You are the representatives of the people of the United States and this resolution is an expression of the people you represent. I will leave this chamber while this matter is debated by this legislative body. When you have reached that consensus, I will be in the President's Room here in the Capitol, awaiting your decision. I will leave the secretary of defense here to answer questions. Remember, time is of the essence."

I watched as the president left the podium and walked back up the aisle and exited the chamber. The pandemonium that broke out when he cleared the chamber must have been ear-shattering with everyone shouting at once. The House Sergeant at Arms attempted to restore order with the aid of the majority leaders from both houses of Congress.

Everyone in the dayroom started talking at once also. A palpable fear ran through the room as everyone contemplated a nuclear war with the Soviets. Fighting commandos was one thing, but how do you defend yourself from an incoming ICBM? The answer, of course, is that you can't. We knew that there was a missile defense shield partially deployed, but it had never been tested under combat conditions. No one had much faith in the shield.

I was worried about Todd lying in bed having just watched this and not being able to get up and do anything. If it was nuclear war, I was going to die with Todd no matter what. The Air Force would not need me if we were going to be obliterated. I intended to keep my promise to the man I loved.

We all heard the phone ringing in the office of the sergeant in charge of the barracks. Everyone became quiet, trying to determine if it was an action call or a routine call. We didn't have to wait long.

"Gentlemen, I just received a phone call from communications notifying us that we are now at Def Con One. You are ordered to report to your duty stations in full uniform and properly armed at once. Let's go. Move it!"

I ran in confusion back to my room. If the president had not made any decisions yet, why were we at Def Con One? That condition meant we were at war and getting ready to launch everything we had. That was almost one hundred missiles, each armed with ten warheads. Our base alone would create total destruction inside the Soviet Union or any other country that was targeted by them. This didn't include all of the other missile bases, the nuclear bombers, or the submarine force that was even now sending target data to their missiles in preparation for launch. And what of the Soviets? Their satellites would be able to tell by our activity at all our bases that we'd gone to the final click on the defense meter.

Again, my thoughts returned to Todd. Since no decision had been made by the president, I would hold off on going to him. My first obligation was to report to duty. After drawing my sidearm, I reported for guard mount at base police headquarters. Sergeant Gray addressed us in formation.

"Okay, listen up. Callahan, you've got the desk. The rest of you men will take your normal stations. We're at Def Con One, which means positive ID on everyone that enters this base including passengers in vehicles. If they are not Air Force, they don't get on base. There is now a weapons-free policy in effect at all secured sites on base. This means the guys guarding all of our nukes on base will shoot anyone seen in their secured areas that aren't supposed to be there. That includes you men. Do not enter any nuclear location until further notice. We should know within an hour or so what the president is going to do.

"If we do launch, that means we are at all-out war. I don't give us a plug nickel's worth of a chance of surviving more than three hours after we launch if that long. You will not call home. You will not call off base. No one is to know what is going on here at Warren. That is part of the war protocol before release of weapons. Once weapons are airborne, you are free to call home, but remember: you will only upset your loved ones more by telling them we have launched. Use your time well, and try to be brave with your family. Chances are they will need comforting and they won't even know that we are weapons away. Use your heads, gentlemen."

"Sergeant, I live on base with my wife. Permission to go home if this happens?"

"Permission granted to all married men with family on base. You single guys will have to make do with phone calls. Callahan, when notified, activate long distance on all gate phones so that they can call home. Police Four, you are on general patrol. All other units disperse to the three base gates and maintain a blockade of the gates. This base is now closed!"

With that, everyone hit the patrol cars as fast as they could. I joined the current desk sergeant on duty and made a fresh pot of coffee. I might as well go out with a caffeine buzz, I thought. After about ten minutes, I looked up at the window at the desk and found Todd staring back at me through the glass. His arm was in a sling, and he looked kinda pale.

"Todd! What are you doing out of bed?" I asked as I rushed down and around to let him into the desk area.

"I listened to the president's address and knew you couldn't get away from here. So I came to you."

"Well, if there are two of you here, I'm heading to my base house to be with my wife and kids. Tell Gray where I'm at," the desk sergeant said.

"Don't do that," Todd said. "They could technically get you for abandoning your post in a time of war. That's a shooting offense. Call Gray on the radio and let him know what you're doing by requesting permission to go."

"Yeah, you're right. I guess I'm not thinking clearly at the moment."

He checked with Sergeant Gray and received permission to go. Gray also said he was en route back to the desk. As soon as the other desk sergeant left, Todd reached up and kissed me deep and hard. I tried not to put any pressure on his shoulder and hugged him back more on the side than directly around his chest.

"I'm glad you could come. I was worried sick about you and not being able to get to you if the end was coming."

I bent forward and kissed him again. When I broke the kiss, I found Sergeant Gray staring at us through the glass. My face drained of color.

"Buzz me in."

I reached down and hit the button that buzzed the lock on the door to the open position so he could get into the secured area. Since the remodeling, the door and entire front of the desk area had been reinforced to make it much harder to breach if there was another attack. The window to the outside had also been taken out and the space bricked up to match the rest of the building.

"Ah, Sergeant Gray. Sir, don't read too much into what you just saw...."

"Be quiet, Callahan. Do you really think I give a shit if you're queer and Todd here is your boyfriend? The entire world is getting ready to fucking explode. I didn't care before this and I sure as hell don't care now if one of my men is gay."

"I don't know what to say," I said meekly.

"Claymore, what are you doing out of the hospital and do they know you're gone?"

"I couldn't just lay in bed while the world blew up, Sergeant Gray; I had to be here in the action. My wound is mostly closed up and healing, so I'm okay. As for the hospital, they have all gone nuts over there and no one knows anything at the moment. Everyone is running around preparing for war without realizing that there will be nothing left that will need medical assistance."

"In other words, you had to be with your boyfriend, right?"

"As a matter of fact, yes. I love Bryce and if the world is going to end, I want to be with him when it does."

"I don't blame you. Okay, call the hospital and let them know you are here. Now that he *is* here, Callahan, can I count on you staying put through the end, if there is one?"

"Totally, Sergeant."

"I'd tell you to carry on, but I'm afraid of what you two might carry on with. Remember, you're on duty, Callahan. Claymore, you might as well act as assisting desk sergeant since you're here. I'm going back out on the road."

"Yes, Sergeant Gray."

Upon notifying base hospital that Todd was here and assisting the desk sergeant, they noted it and hung up. They didn't seem to care much that Todd was gone, which frankly didn't surprise either one of us.

The phone rang, interrupting the reunion.

"Desk sergeant."

"Colonel Drake here, Wing Command Post. The president has formally put us on a war footing. The Soviets have forty hours left to comply with the Congressional demand that they retake their base from the rebels. If they fail to do so, we have orders to launch all missiles should they respond to the one we launch to take out Pinsk South missile base. We'll get the call from NORAD in the event we detect launches from the Soviet Union. Implement all of your standard operating procedures for a state of war."

When I acknowledged the order, the call was disconnected. By the look on my face, Todd could tell that something was wrong.

"Have we launched? Is that the call?"

"No, we launch only if the Soviets respond to us taking out the rebel base."

I pulled down the Def Con One SOP book and went through the checklist. Most of the procedures had already been implemented. All security policemen had been recalled to base at the beginning of ground hostilities. Todd took care of one or two things while I radioed for Sergeant Gray to call in. Next, I picked up the phone and called the commanding officer of the security police squadron and notified him of the Wing Command Post's order. The commanding general would have had a call first from the Command Post prior to me getting the call.

Once I briefed the sergeant, I was caught up on my duties for the moment. I brought Todd coffee and we were able to talk at length for once without any interruptions. Everyone was deep in their own thoughts as to the possible ending of their lives and the lives of their families. Everyone was proud to serve the nation as a member of the Air Force, but ultimately, our position in the Air Force was exactly what would guarantee our quick deaths in the event of war.

As the hour began to approach dawn, Todd decided he wanted us to be able to sleep together today since we didn't know how many more days there would be.

"When you can leave, let's hit the hospital, let them check my bandages, give me a shot and a couple of pills, and then we can go back to the barracks. With everything in a state of tension and worry, I doubt if they will put up much of a fuss."

"Are you sure that's wise? I mean, we shouldn't take any risks with your health."

"Would you listen to yourself? You're worried about my shoulder when we might have Soviet ICBMs raining down on our heads in a little over—what—thirty-eight hours from now?"

"Okay. Point well taken."

The major entered the building and went directly to his office after asking me for an update. He didn't even ask why Todd was out of the hospital. The day shift followed shortly after the major, and I was relieved from my post.

We hitched a ride from day shift and were able to see a doctor pretty quickly at the base hospital. They looked Todd over and found no reason why he couldn't have leave to go to the barracks as long as he came back for another check in twelve hours. They didn't give him a shot, though; pills were dispensed to control the pain, and they gave him more antibiotics for infection prevention. While we were at the hospital, we took advantage of the cafeteria there and ate breakfast. Once that was done, we headed to the barracks and got into bed.

"Todd, I'm scared. What will it be like if we get hit by a nuke?"

"That's the thing, Bryce. We won't really have any time to think about it once they hit. Everything around here will be vaporized if we are ground zero for the warheads. A good chunk of Cheyenne will be gone also. The population that doesn't die immediately will begin to die of radiation poisoning unless they get away from air currents transporting the radioactive dust particles. We won't feel any pain because they told us in previous briefings that it will happen so quickly, our brains won't register much of anything."

"All of this is so incredible. How did we get to this point as the human race? Why can't we ever seem to settle our differences without massive loss of life? We are both young, like many men in the Soviet military, and yet we all are going to die way before we should because the idiots that run our governments won't settle this quickly."

"Well, we have a little less than two days for sure, so let's just hold tight to each other and cherish what we've found in this place. I really never expected to find a guy I would fall in love with. As I often mentioned to you, most guys just wanted me for my equipment, but not for who I am as a person. You're different in that respect, and it's like fate is making us pay for falling in love. The only other option we have is to desert and that isn't even thinkable. So we are left with the sole option of praying that war will be avoided and staying as close to each other as we can."

I snuggled in closer to my man while trying not to hurt his shoulder. I was tired, and so was Todd after having taken his pills. We finally drifted off to sleep with thoughts of mushroom clouds over Cheyenne.

We were woken up at just after 1400 hours by the barracks sergeant, who told us to report to the base hangar in dress blues. We had no idea what we were to do, but the order included Todd. As we got dressed, we wondered if we were forming up to receive a VIP who was landing and we were acting as honor guard. The only thing that didn't make sense was that Todd's arm was still in a sling and was supposed to be for at least another day.

When we left our room and headed down into the entranceway to the barracks, we found the other members of our team that had landed at the missile site and engaged the commandos. It started to dawn on everyone that since we were in dress blues, it was probably a medal ceremony. I personally thought that with the world about to end, medals were the last thing I cared about. But the Air Force thought differently. Outside were two blue Air Force sedans waiting to take us to the hanger, which was a good distance from our barracks. The driver was tight-lipped about our purpose for going there and we finally gave up trying to pump him for information.

After pulling up and getting out of the car, we found a hangar full of people waiting on us. As we entered, the major came up to us and returned our salutes.

"Gentlemen, this is an awards ceremony. The morning after the firefight, the general put you all in for medals as a result of your successful defense of Bravo-David Four. Take up your positions between the national colors and the Air Force flag and rest at ease."

We did as we were told. After a couple of moments, the general and his immediate staff along with the base commander entered the hangar and the area was called to attention. The general took the podium and began to speak.

"It is my distinct pleasure today to award various medals to the security policemen who engaged enemy commandos in defense of missile silo Bravo-David Four. After landing from the air in response to an alarm, they were met with fierce resistance from seven Russian commandos on the ground. As a direct result of engagement of the enemy, five of the six security policemen were wounded or injured in some fashion. The one airman not injured was requested to remove a device found on top of the silo, which was meant to crack the shell and release radiation into the atmosphere. The airman in question has received no training whatsoever in the handling of explosives as this is not a part of general security police training. He successfully removed the explosive device from the silo and carried it far enough away to protect both the missile and his fellow airmen. He had a total of about four minutes to accomplish this before the device was set to explode. We have since determined that the device was made with blocks of Semtex, a plastic explosive. There was more than a sufficient quantity to have destroyed the casing around the missile. For these acts on this date, the following medals are hereby awarded:

"All six airmen are hereby awarded the Air Force Combat Action Medal, which is awarded for engaging in combat in the air or on the ground as part of their official duty.

"All six airmen are hereby awarded the Air Force Commendation Medal for sustained acts of heroism while in contact with the enemy in combat.

"Five of the six airmen are hereby awarded the Purple Heart for injury or wounds sustained while engaged in combat with the enemy.

"All six airmen are hereby awarded a Presidential Unit Citation for action in combat.

"Airman Bryce Callahan is hereby awarded the Bronze Star for bravery in a combat situation in not only engaging the enemy in a firefight, but by knowingly risking his life by removing an unknown explosive device set to go off on top of a missile.

"Finally, after heavy combat and without any backup, Airman Bryce Callahan defended his post from attack by three Soviet commandos at the base police desk. In defending his post, Airman Callahan killed in action all attacking forces and is hereby awarded the Silver Star for conspicuous bravery in the face of the enemy."

The general, with an aide carrying a flat wooden box, left the podium and stood in front of each airman one at a time. After taking each medal from the box, he pinned the medals on the outside of each airman's Class A uniform jacket. We each in turn saluted the general after he finished awarding our particular medals.

The ceremony was abbreviated and the passing of the troops in front of the general and the medal honorees was done away with so that all could return quickly to their duties. The major gave each of us the ribbons for our uniforms that represented the medals awarded so that they could be added to our dress uniforms. I hoped we had an opportunity to wear them again.

The total time taken for the ceremony was thirty-five minutes. We were back in our barracks by 1500 hours, and had to decide whether or not to go back to bed, or stay up and just go to work. Todd decided to go over to the hospital early to have a checkup, which also gave him the opportunity to stay in dress blues and show off his new medals. I went back to bed with the promise that Todd would be back in plenty of time to wake me up to return to duty.

BY the time I had once again taken up my position as desk sergeant for the base police squadron, we had twenty-six hours left before the launch deadline. I had never seen the guys so on edge before, not even when we were expecting the commando attack. A couple of the married guys called off sick and were ordered to report to sick call at the base hospital at once. We all knew they weren't sick, but understood why they wanted to be with their families. The order to sick call was to cover the sergeant's ass should the major make a big deal about it.

The base remained locked down with no movement either on or off base. All personnel on base were confined to base for the duration. Anyone not already on base was AWOL and would be dealt with after the crisis passed. The movie theater and bowling alley were closed. Basically, unless you were on duty, you remained in your respective housing. Warren Air Force Base was like a ghost town with the exception of the security and police patrols and the men manning the gates to the base.

We had been notified that the body of the last commando had been found by search parties. Apparently the dumb bastard stepped on an adult rattlesnake in the dark, and was struck. Ivan remembered everything to bring to a hot party with the exception of a snake-bite kit.

I thought back to my own encounter with a snake and was glad it had a distinctly different outcome.

Todd was once again keeping me company on the desk with the permission of Sergeant Gray and the hospital. He took care of the coffee for everyone while I took care of the nightly report. The stillness began to get to everyone and nerves were frayed. The highway that passes by the main gate was eerily silent as even the civilians were staying close to home or had fled the area, realizing our potential to be hit. The sky was clear in a sort of mocking way with a nearly full moon and a light breeze. Was the moon trying to tell us that we would actually see the incoming missiles due to the clarity of the night sky?

The rest of the shift was met with total silence. There were no calls for police service, no alarms, and no attempts to enter the base legally or illegally. The only thing maintaining our attention was the minute sweep hand on our watches and clocks.

Just after 0400 hours, Sergeant Gray came in off patrol and brought us two box lunches. It was better than nothing. He got a cup of coffee and sat down in the only other empty chair at the desk.

"Well, tell me guys. How long have you two been a couple?"

"A few weeks after I arrived at Warren. Todd was assigned to me as my training and security partner and things just went on from there."

"Claymore, you been with anyone else here before Callahan?"

"No, Sergeant Gray, I haven't been. I'm not even sure if there are other gay men here at Warren."

Gray laughed and replied, "Oh, one thing you can be assured of is that you two aren't the only lilies in the flower field. I do believe, however, that you are the only couple I know of or have heard of around here. Times are changing with the newer guys. They are more accepting of gays; but the old-timers? Not in a million years. They will always be against you guys and there's no changing their minds either."

"Why is that, do you think, Sergeant?" I asked.

"Well, stereotypes for one thing. You know that Bronze Star and Silver Star you just won? In their views a gay man would never be able to win a medal for bravery. They are products of their own era and they believe gays are cowards. They also believe you'll be busy sucking cock in the foxhole instead of killing the enemy. If they had the slightest idea about both you guys, they wouldn't give you a break for anything."

"And how would they explain away our new medals?" Todd asked.

"They would say it was either a fluke that you got them, or that gays higher up were making sure you fellows got your share of glory. It's a damn shame they're so blind. I predict it's only a matter of a couple more years, and you all will be able to serve openly and there won't be anything they can do about it. In fact, it will create an exodus of senior enlisted types into retirement as a result. Frankly, I'm not too sure that isn't a blessing in disguise. I've never had any problems from you two. I wish I could say that about all my men. You show up for duty on time, your uniforms are together, and you do your job. What more can I ask as a flight sergeant?"

"We are here to do a job like everyone else. On down time, the other guys go out and socialize and have fun. We don't have the same ability to socialize with other gay men. The fact that Todd and I met each other is really something that surprised us both since neither had thought it would happen."

"Well, just do your jobs and you'll never have a problem out of me. But if this crisis blows over and we don't end up as minute particles, make sure you keep your relationship top secret. You live off base normally, right?"

"Yep, have for a couple months now. Once we can get out of the barracks, we'll move back to our place."

"Good, much better that way. Okay, I'm going to do a check of the three gates. By the way, make an entry into the shift report that Claymore volunteered to assist with desk duties since he still cannot go on normal patrol."

CHAPTER 10

THE shift had ended and we repeated our routine with the hospital and back to the barracks. This time we headed to the television room to catch up on the news and find out if we were closer to war or moving away from it. We weren't the only ones. Most of the night shift were fixated on the CNN morning news hour.

The Soviets were still rattling their sabers at the U.S. in an attempt to keep us from launching at the rebel base. They reported that they had troops moving into the area and that an all-out assault would take place as soon as the troops were in position. As the Soviet television commentator rattled on, a friend of mine who worked in the missile division came in and sat down next to me. After watching for a few moments, he leaned over and whispered quietly to me.

"I just found out Warren will be the base that launches the single missile to take out the rebel base. That makes it a certainty that we will be heavily targeted when they respond to the attack. But keep it quiet as I'm not sure if they are going to tell everyone or not."

"Okay. Thanks, Fred."

"Can you take a walk with me for a moment?"

"Sure. Where to? We're really not supposed to be out walking around, as you know, unless we're on duty."

"How about your room?"

"Okay. Let's go."

I leaned over to tell Todd that I was going back to the room for a minute as Fred wanted to talk to me. As we walked, I noticed Fred seemed stressed out even more than the rest of us. I wasn't too good at counseling and if that's what he needed, he should go to the chaplain or someone at the hospital.

We went into my room and sat down. "So, what's up, Fred? You look like shit."

"Well, Bryce, it's pretty probable that we're all gonna be blown to hell within a matter of hours and so I thought I would tell you something before that happens. You know, kinda like there's nothing to lose."

"Okay. What is it?" I asked with a chuckle as I felt he was being a bit dramatic.

"Look, I like you a lot, Bryce; I have since you first arrived on base. Can you deal with me liking you, or does it freak you out?"

"Why would our being friends freak me out, Fred?"

"I don't think you understand what I'm saying. I really like you, Bryce, and I want to show you how much."

"What, you want to buy me something or what?" I asked, getting a little nervous.

"No, I wanna blow you. I'm gay and I want to have sex with you before we all die."

"Oh. Okay, I see what you mean. Well, I'm very flattered, Fred, but I'm afraid that's not gonna be possible. We can still remain friends, but it has to be platonic."

"So, you're not gay then?"

I didn't know quite how to respond to that question. I didn't want to lie to him but I also remembered what Sergeant Gray had told Todd and me at the desk. "Fred, I don't want to get into all that. Look, just please accept that nothing sexual is possible between us and just enjoy our friendship. I'm not going to rat you out, or dump you as a friend, so don't worry about that."

"I didn't think I would get lucky for once, but I had to try. Do you hate me?"

"No, I don't hate you at all. I'm sorry that I can't give you what you want. Be careful in looking for another guy to hook up with. Don't get yourself turned in to OSI or you'll end up under investigation."

He got up and shook my hand and left the room rather dejectedly. I felt so sorry for him; I knew it was difficult to be gay and have to be in the closet with the knowledge that you might not ever find a partner. He was a friend, but now I did have a partner that I had to remain true to. I loved Todd. I debated on whether or not to even tell him about the conversation with Fred.

When I returned to the television dayroom, everyone was pretty much in the same spots they had been in when I had left. Todd looked at me and smiled and turned back to the television. The big discussion among the talking heads was that there were only thirteen hours left until the deadline set by Congress passed. As I looked at the clock, I realized I would be on duty as desk sergeant when the launching of the solo missile was to take place. In fact, everything that could evolve would occur on my very next shift. My blood ran cold at the thought of dying in just a few hours' time.

"Todd, I'm going to bed. If all hell is gonna break loose tonight, I might as well be awake to enjoy it!"

AS I stripped off my clothes and climbed into bed, Todd entered the room. "I figured I would join you since this may be our last time in bed together."

I watched him slowly remove his clothes and found myself becoming aroused. When he dropped his uniform pants, he was naked. He didn't bother to wear any underwear, which I thought must have been very uncomfortable with the size of his endowment. He took the sling off, which he wasn't supposed to do until another twenty-four hours had passed, and slipped under the sheets with me. I was now fully erect and wanting to make love.

As Todd smiled at me, my hand wandered over his body and down to his dick. There I found his sleeping anaconda and began to massage it. Slowly he became fully erect and I began to jerk him up and down after kicking the sheet off us. It was difficult to maneuver in the bunk bed we shared, as it was only meant to hold one guy. I had to be careful not to put any strain on his shoulder area by moving him around a lot, so I gingerly slid down between his legs.

"Make it slow and easy, will you, doll face?" he asked. I once again began the daunting task of giving oral sex to the man I loved, which normally would be a simple matter. With Todd, of course, it was work. After I began to go down on him, I heard a groan that I took for pleasure but quickly learned was one of pain. I stopped what I was doing and looked up.

"What is it? Are you in pain?"

"Yeah, damn it. When you started sucking, my body tensed up from the pleasure, and that pulled on the muscles in my shoulder and chest. I think no matter how you do it, the same thing is going to happen. I don't think I could take an orgasm either. I'm sorry, Todd. I know how much you enjoy working on Mr. Happy down there."

I laughed out loud at his use of one of his pet names for his dick. Here he was lying with a throbbing erection and no way to relieve him of the condition. I frowned, patted his dick, and slid back onto my side next to him.

"I'm sorry I can't give you the pleasure you deserve. But it's more important for you not to be in pain or break open the stitches because of our fooling around. That would be hard to explain at the hospital."

It was Todd's turn to laugh. "Yeah, I don't think they would be ready for that explanation. Okay; I can give you a hand, though. Interested?"

"No. If you can't get off, then I don't want to. This crisis will end, and we will have a million chances to give each other pleasure. Let's just go to sleep now. We don't know what tonight is going to bring."

What's wrong with me?, I asked myself. That's twice in the space of an hour I'd turned down sex. I had no intention of making that a habit!

EVEN as tired as we were, we ended up waking early and got out of bed just after 1500 hours. We threw on some civvies and went down to the television room to see the latest news. As usual, the room was crowded, but we managed to find two seats together.

The television was tuned in to CNN and we listened as the talking head droned on about the approaching deadline.

"Soviet troops continue their assault on the rebel missile base known as Pinsk South. The fighting has been raging for over five hours now, with both sides apparently sustaining heavy casualties. All this is going on as Washington monitors the situation with an eye to the approaching deadline, which is just a little over four hours from now. The question of the hour is: Will the United States carry out its threat to launch a missile to take out the rebel base if it remains in their hands at zero hour, even while the Soviets are engaged in battle to retake the base?"

"We couldn't be stupid enough to launch a missile at that base while they're actually trying to retake it, could we?" I asked Todd.

"I would tend to think we would let them handle it at this point. There's no need to start World War Three as long as they are dealing with the crisis. But, who knows. We're on duty in a little less than two hours. We should start getting ready and then go eat."

AFTER eating and as we approached the armory on foot, Todd said, "If we don't make it to sunrise, I want you to know that I've been very happy with you over these weeks we've been together as a couple. You're a unique man who is very sweet, sexy, smart, and who obviously has good taste in men."

I had to laugh at the last part of his statement. "Well, Todd, you already know how I feel about you. We have to hope that there will be many more tomorrows and that we will have a chance to plan out our lives and look to the future."

I checked my sidearm out of the armory, and we headed over to the base police station. Sergeant Gray was waiting on us, but I noticed that none of the married guys were present for guard mount. We were the last to arrive and I took my place in line as Todd sat down in the other room.

"Okay, now that everyone is here, let's begin. This is going to be a very tense shift. As you know, the deadline is drawing near for us to launch a missile to take out the rebel base in the Soviet Union. We don't know what effect the attack on the base by Soviet forces will have on the deadline. Personally, I hope we let them do everything they can to take that base out of action. For this shift, everything is the same as last night. Callahan, you have the desk; the rest of you will have gate duty as you did last night. I will be the only patrol out as we are concentrating on the gates, and the married guys are off with their families. If we need them, they will respond within five minutes to the armory. As soon as we know anything about the Soviet situation, I will have Callahan let all gates and units know. You men who are covering Gates Two and Three: Stay in your patrol cars in case you are needed for something. Make sure the chains are secured on both gates at the beginning of your shift. And stay awake; it may be a long night!"

With that, everyone scattered for their assigned posts. I relieved the day-shift sergeant and took over the desk. I quickly started my shift report, hoping that it would not be the last time I did so. Todd put on fresh coffee and we settled into our chairs, waiting for the phone to light up from the Wing Command Post. That was the way I would learn of any significant event.

"I guess, Todd, we'll be here if we have a mutual launch when the shit hits the fan. The post orders call for me to transfer calls to the basement and take a portable radio with me and transfer operations downstairs. I'm not sure what good that will do us, but that's what the procedures direct."

"Should I go down now and unlock the room and turn on lights and equipment in case we get the word to do so?"

"Good idea. We have no prisoners in the cell block so there is no reason not to have the room activated and the door left open."

As I watched Todd leave the secured area of the desk and head down the hallway to the door that led to the basement, a tear welled up in my eye. I had come to love this man so much and to have the very strong chance of losing him this very night was almost more than my emotional state could deal with. It just wasn't fair.

I had calls from all three gates telling me everything was secured at the start of the shift, which was routine. I noted this fact in my report. Todd rejoined me a moment later and announced that the emergency desk operation was ready to go active. I pulled down the SOP book for operating under those conditions to have it ready to go quickly with us. I also pulled out our hidden weapons to go as well. That was all we would need to take with us, as most everything else was already down in the alternate desk location.

The deadline passed without the phone ringing and we began to relax somewhat. I started to receive calls from the direct lines at the three gates asking me if I had heard anything, to which I replied that I hadn't. As I took another sip of my coffee, the phone rang again, and I cursed the gate guards for being bothersome. When I leaned forward to get the phone, I saw that it was the Wing Command Post. With my heart in my throat I answered.

"Callahan."

"Callahan, this is Wing Command Post. We have been notified that a missile has been launched from the rebel base in the Soviet Union. It launched approximately four minutes ago and is a little over eight thousand miles away. Trajectory cannot be determined. Suggest you transfer your operation to alternate desk area."

The line went dead as the officer had hung up. I jumped up and quickly grabbed the radio mic and announced, "Base police desk transferring to alternate post location." This notified Sergeant Gray and any unit monitoring my radio frequency that we were at war.

"Todd, grab that stuff and let's get downstairs ASAP."

As we ran down the hallway toward the door to the basement, Todd asked if we had multiple incoming missiles. I told him what the

Command Post had told me and we practically jumped down the staircase to the bottom floor of the building and ran into the alternate desk location, which was in the northeast corner of the building. We set up the few remaining things to be done just in time for the phone to begin ringing. It was the gates all calling in at one time. They had been told at guard mount that I would keep them posted.

One by one I relayed to them what I had been told. Sergeant Gray called in from his house and advised that he stopped in to be with his wife for a moment and asked to be briefed. I relayed to him what Command Post said, and he thanked me and said he would be back on the road in five minutes.

I next phoned the squadron commander and informed him of the message from Command Post. He thanked me, and the call was terminated. The only thing I had to do now was wait for an update from the Command Post. I knew that NORAD was tracking the Soviet missile and would be able to project an impact point fairly quickly based on trajectory.

The phone rang again. It was the Command Post and I answered the phone with great dread. "Callahan, Command Post. We have launched one of our missiles to take out the Pinsk South missile base. This is probably the beginning of the end." The line went dead.

I turned to Todd and kissed him quickly and told him what the Command Post had said. I dialed up Sergeant Gray at his residence and notified him of the latest news. He advised me he would say goodbye to his wife and was en route back to my location. I picked up my direct lines to the main gate and advised them of what I had been told. I didn't want to put it out over the air, so I did not advise the guys at Gates Two and Three, who remained in their patrol cars.

Todd moved over next to me and put his arm around me and we sat there in silence. We would be able to hear anyone coming down the stairs so that we could separate before we were seen. I leaned into Todd and kissed him again and began to tear up once more. This time Todd, my big, strong macho man, did likewise.

"Well, so much for making long-term plans for Italy, my love," said Todd with a frown.

"Well, if it wasn't meant to be, it wasn't meant to be. The one thing that comforts me is that you are here with me and no matter what happens we will either live together, or die together. Fucking politicians!"

We heard Sergeant Gray arrive and start down the staircase. Todd and I separated and got ourselves back together again quickly. The sergeant walked into the office and just looked at us for a moment.

"Callahan, you might be the luckiest man on duty. At least you've got the one you love with you. What have you told the other men?"

"I advised the main gate by landline of what's going on, but not the other two gates. I didn't know if you wanted me to put out on the airwaves that we have launched a missile."

"Fuck, I don't know what to do at this point. It's not like this has ever been covered in training before! Tell you what. Have them go into the gatehouse at Two and Three and call in here. When they call, brief them. Better do it now."

After using the portable radio to give the directions, I received phone calls from both gates in just a matter of a few moments. I quickly relayed the latest information and they asked what they should do. Sergeant Gray ordered them to maintain their posts until relieved or told otherwise.

"How long will it take the incoming missile to hit its target in the U.S.?" I asked him.

"It's a thirty-minute flight time for either missile to impact. Since they launched first, their missile will hit first, followed closely by ours.

Since you've not been notified that multiple launches have occurred, it seems that we are dealing with only two missiles with maybe eleven warheads. Looking at my watch, I would say that the Soviet missile is crossing the North Pole and inbound to the U.S. with an impact of about twelve minutes. I guess...."

The phone rang, making me jump out of my seat. "Callahan."

"This is Colonel Rodriguez, Wing Command Post. We have successfully terminated the inbound flight of the Soviet ICBM and have sent a destruct signal to our own ICBM, which is over the North Pole heading toward Soviet airspace."

"What does that mean, that we have terminated the inbound flight?"

"It means our missile defense shield worked and we were able to destroy the hostile missile. We are waiting from further word from the Pentagon and other sources to determine our next steps."

The phone went dead. I relayed the news to Sergeant Gray and Todd, both of whom broke out into big smiles. The crisis wasn't over yet, but at least there were no armed ICBMs in flight at the moment. We all breathed a little easier.

"Let our guys know at once."

I went through the same process as before to notify all on-duty base police and security forces of the latest situation report. A palpable sense of relief was exhibited by all I relayed the good news to. I also cautioned them that we were not out of the woods yet. We still had the president's determination to neutralize the threat. Tonight's launch from the rebel base would only reinforce the views of the hawks in the administration.

"Have you notified the squadron commander yet of the latest?" asked Sergeant Gray.

"Actually, the Command Post told me they are relaying situation reports directly to him. So, he is one less thing on my list to take care of each time we have a change in status."

"Okay, well, transfer your operation back upstairs to the normal desk sergeant's area. But if we get another missile alert, head back down here again."

After getting resettled into my normal duty station, we made new coffee and once again began the vigil for the next action to take place in this dance of death. I had to wait more than an hour before I once again had an update from Command Post.

"Callahan, Command Post here. The Soviets have retaken the rebel base about twenty minutes ago and have declared it secure and back under Soviet national command authority. They are backing down their war footing and we are waiting for our National Defense Command Authority to back us down to Def Con Two at least. It looks like, at least for now, the crisis will pass and we can return to normal life. We will let you know as soon as we receive any further word or orders."

Sergeant Gray was still present when the latest notification came in and he was visibly relieved. "Callahan, I'll let our men know in person. Make sure your report is up to date on everything that has happened tonight. Radio me as soon as you receive confirmation of a reduction in Def Con status."

Gray left the office and I once again hugged and kissed my lover. "Well, it looks like we're not going to go up in flames tonight after all, my darling!" I said to Todd. He just smiled and kissed me quickly once again.

IT was another four hours before I received a follow-up call from the Wing Command Post. The Pentagon had flash-ordered all military commands to downgrade the Def Con status from Def Con One to Def Con Two. This was still one step higher than our normal status, but it sent a clear signal that we were no longer preparing for imminent war. By the time I was notified of this fact, it was almost 0200 hours and we were starving. Sergeant Gray sent one of the patrol units to the desk so that both Todd and I could actually take a car and go to the chow hall for a decent meal. It was the first time I'd been able to do that in well over two weeks.

We returned to my duty station and the rest of the shift passed without any further tension on the world stage. At 0500 hours, the squadron commander issued an order to relax gate control of the base. We would return to a more normal routine commencing with the very next shift. I also hoped that we would soon return to our normal duty hours and be able to live off base once more. When you have a partner, living in the barracks is definitely not fun. I couldn't wait until Todd and I could reclaim our home.

I finished up my shift report and was relieved by the incoming desk sergeant. As I was getting ready to go, the major came out of his office and called me over to him.

"Callahan, you did an outstanding job all through this increased Def Con condition. You can look for your next stripe as soon as you have enough time in grade to be promoted."

"Thank you, sir. I appreciate that very much. May I ask, sir, when we might return to our regular shifts, with a three-shift duty day here on base?"

"Well, not until we go back to Def Con Three, which I'm hoping will be just a matter of another day or so. I know it's been hard on everyone these past couple of weeks, but especially here and out in the field. I suppose you also want to live off base again?"

"Most definitely, sir. I can't say I like barracks life at all. Way too noisy, no privacy, and the accommodations aren't that good, sir."

After he stopped chuckling, he replied, "I'll see what I can do about that also. Carry on, airman."

"Yes, sir. Have a good day."

I joined Todd outside the building and we walked the 150 feet to the base armory where I checked my sidearm back in. We then headed directly to the hospital with one of the day units so that Todd could have his bandages changed and a checkup of how he was healing. He said he felt pretty good, but that could have just been the pain pills he took a half-hour earlier.

CHAPTER 11

TODD was given a clean bill of health and officially discharged from the hospital. He was able to get rid of the sling, but was restricted to light duty for another week. This was great news as it meant that our lives might be returning to some level of normalcy.

Within another day, our defense condition was lowered back to Def Con Three, which was as low as we ever went. The rest of the military returned to Def Con Four. We were allowed to move back off base, and we returned to normal eight-hour shifts, with two days a week off. Life was getting sweet once again.

It was great to return to our house where we could walk around naked if we wanted to without worrying about what anyone else thought. We cooked dinner every night we felt like it, and partied on the weekends. Since we were no longer stuck on a permanent mid-night shift, but rather rotated through the three different shifts, we were able to work the day shift once every three weeks and have evenings free.

Our robust sex life returned to us with a vengeance. We had a lot of tension and hormones backed up since the world went crazy and we enjoyed each other at the drop of a hat. I was actually becoming quite good at handling Todd's endowment, which resulted in even better sex for him. If the day ever came where "don't ask, don't tell" was repealed, we would exchange rings as a sign of our love and search out other gay couples on base. We needed a social structure to go along with our relationship. We wanted to share our happiness with others and not have to always keep it a secret. There were rumblings about repealing the repressive policy and we could only hope that the new administration would follow through and make our lives even better.

Upon occasion, we heard whispers behind our backs from some of the others that we were more than just roommates, but we refused to let it concern us. Our squadron commander never bothered us and in fact seemed to look out after me. Ever since the firefight with the Soviet commandos and the resulting medals, the major always appeared friendly to me whenever we met. It almost seemed that being awarded the Bronze and Silver Star was a security policy for us, making everyone leave us alone.

Everything was going along fairly well until the day I was called into the Office of Special Investigations, or the OSI. I had no idea what they wanted so I was puzzled as I sat in their outer office waiting to be told what I was doing there.

"Airman Callahan, come in."

As I entered the inner office, I found two OSI agents sitting behind a desk. I was told to sit down and make myself comfortable. I was offered coffee, which I declined. Then it started.

"Do you know why you're here, Callahan?" asked the younger of the two agents.

"Nope. I have no idea whatsoever. Why am I here?"

"First things first. I'm Agent Milson, and this is Agent Parker. You have the right to remain silent, and you have the right to be represented by an attorney during and after questioning. You may give up your rights and answer our questions and if you do, you can stop at any time you feel the need to. Do you understand your rights?"

Okay, I was now in shock. These clowns were reading me my rights! What in the hell was going on?

"Yes, I understand my rights, since I give them out to people I place under arrest. Now what the hell is all this about?"

"Callahan, you are under investigation for being a homosexual. We have received information that you are carrying on a homosexual relationship with a Sergeant Todd Claymore, which started shortly after you arrived here at Warren. Do you deny this?"

Before I answered, I noticed that the older agent had put a tape recorder on the desk, recording everything I said.

By instinct and little else, I answered, "Of course I deny it. It's a lie! Who gave you this information?"

"Well, first, we can't reveal our sources unless this goes to a court-martial. Second, you should really consider cooperating with us so that we can help you."

"Help me! You're trying to fuck me over and you want to help me? How do you propose to help me?"

"We can get you psychological help before you are discharged to deal with your homosexuality. We want you to get well. After all, we're not monsters."

After my jaw dropped open, I laughed out loud. I couldn't help myself, it just happened. This seemed to piss off both agents.

"There is nothing funny about your being a homosexual! You have security clearances that give you access to top-secret information as well as weapon cards that give you access to firearms at the base armory. You are a security threat."

"Bullshit! First of all, I don't believe that a gay person is any more of a security threat than any other member of the Air Force. Do you guys realize that there has never been a single case in American military history where a gay person betrayed this country? Do you also know how many times betrayal by heterosexual members of all branches of the military and CIA *has* occurred? Don't' tell me that homosexuals constitute a security threat. And if a threat ever arises from the gay community it will be because of witch hunts like this one!"

"Callahan, how is it that you even know these facts?"

"I like to read, and anything to do with security issues I make sure to read. I ask you again, what information do you have that leads you to believe this?"

"We can't get specific, Callahan. Are you sure you don't want to cooperate with us and make it easier on yourself? If we have to go for a court-martial, you could end up with a bad-conduct discharge, which would screw up the rest of your life."

"Yeah, well, I'll take that chance. Do whatever you have to do with this shit."

"Okay, as of now, your security clearances are suspended, and your weapons cards are revoked. You need to turn those over to me now."

"You're joking! How do I work without a weapon or security clearance?"

"As of now, you are suspended from your security police duties. You will report to your administrative officer, Captain Blackman, for further disposition. Proceedings to discharge you from the Air Force will be commenced immediately. Now turn over your weapons cards."

I got up, pulled my wallet out, and practically threw my weapons cards at the two smiling agents sitting before me. I had to turn over each card to the armory in order to get a weapon and without the cards, I could not get a weapon. They shoved a paper in front of me that said that I had been advised of my rights and told me to sign it. After signing it, they asked me if I would give them permission to search my off-base housing immediately.

"I would like to consult an attorney first," I angrily replied.

"In that case, it won't be necessary. You may go," the agent said while pointing to the rear door of the building.

I got up and instead opened the door to the outside office to the front of the building and found Todd sitting in a chair waiting to come in next. "No. This way out, please. Do not talk to anyone in the outer office."

Ignoring the directive, I said to Todd, "They just asked to search our off-base home and I told them I wanted an attorney first." One of the two agents grabbed me by the arm and began to pull me back into the office so they could shove me out the back door. I shook off his arm and squared off against him.

"Don't fucking touch me ever again, understand?"

I turned around and walked out the front door of the building. I had hoped that Todd would pick up on my demeanor and realize that I had told them nothing and offered no cooperation.

As I headed toward the squadron admin officer's office, I became more and more furious with each step I took. Fear tinged my mood as well. Did I want Todd and me to be discharged? It would be one way for us to live our lives without fear and plan for the future. It didn't take me long to realize that it was far more than just whether or not we left the Air Force; it was whether or not we were going to let the bastards force us to leave.

I was also gravely concerned about Todd and what they were doing to him in that office. He was almost a hundred percent healed from the bullet wound, but he was still on painkillers and I hoped that wouldn't affect his judgment.

After arriving at the Admin building, I made my way to the captain's office and found his clerk's office outside. When I said I was ordered to report to the captain, the sergeant behind the desk pulled out a file, obviously expecting my arrival. I assumed that Todd would shortly follow in these same footsteps.

"You don't actually need to see the captain himself. Please read this and sign it at the bottom when you've finished," he said after handing me a letter.

The letter informed me that I was being processed for a discharge under Air Force Manual 39-12, for being gay. I looked up at the sergeant and asked in an even tone: "I've only just been accused of this and the Air Force is already trying to get rid of me?"

"It's procedure. This reassigns you to the disciplinary barracks pending discharge. Please understand that I have nothing to do with this matter other than implementing the procedures. I'm not the OSI."

"I'm not signing anything until I consult with an attorney—and a civilian attorney at that. Right now, I don't trust anything Air Force."

"You will be called in by the captain and ordered to sign this if you don't sign it now. This isn't an admission of anything other than that I have told you that you are being processed for discharge. You really don't have the right to refuse to sign this form."

"Well, you'll forgive me if I rely on legal counsel's advice first before doing anything regarding this matter."

I got up and walked out of the office in a fury. I pushed open the door and walked right by the captain without even saluting. I had even forgotten to put on my cap.

"Airman, what's wrong?" the captain shouted at me as I began to walk away.

I stopped and turned around, realizing that I hadn't rendered the required salute and expected a boatload of shit for that.

"Sorry, sir. I'm just really upset right now and didn't realize that you were there."

"What's wrong? Did you just get a letter of reprimand or an Article Fifteen?"

"No, sir. I was just informed that I am being discharged from the Air Force!"

"For what?"

"For being gay!"

"Come into my office, please."

We walked back into the captain's office where the sergeant just had to say, "I told you so."

I shot him a "go fuck yourself" look and went into the captain's office.

"Okay, tell me what this is all about," the captain said.

"Well, sir, I assumed that you would already know about this since your office is processing this thing."

"Bryce, I often don't know about the details of these things until after they are initiated. Then I get a report from Sergeant Killeen in my outer office and that's how I find out what's going on."

I gave the captain the full history of what had just occurred in the OSI office and my abject horror of going from receiving the Bronze and Silver Star one day, to being directed to report to the squadron disciplinary barracks shortly thereafter. I told him how this was going to screw up my life after the Air Force and that we were still living in the Middle Ages.

"Okay, let me look into this whole thing. In the meantime, you do not have to report to the disciplinary barracks. In fact, with your skills as desk sergeant, I need you here in my office to handle administrative matters."

"Won't that be a bit awkward under the circumstances?"

"You can work on everything but discharge proceedings. That leaves all the letters of reprimand and the like. You might be surprised at how many of those letters are given out."

"Yes, sir. I accept, of course. But I have a favor to ask of you."

"Oh? I thought I had just done you one?"

"Yes, sir, more than you will ever realize. However, I expect to see my supposed lover walking in any moment after he tells the OSI to go pound sand up their collective asses. Can he also not be sent to the disciplinary barracks? He's a good man who is dedicated to the Air Force and does not deserve the humiliation of being assigned with drug addicts, disciplinary problems, and mental cases."

"Yes, of course. I know of Sergeant Claymore and I'll see to it that he is put to good use."

"You have my gratitude for being understanding and compassionate, sir. Thank you."

"Very well. Look, take the rest of the day off and report at 0800 hours. I suggest you get an attorney or whatever you're gonna do about this other matter."

"Yes, sir. I intend to get civilian counsel to represent both Todd and me."

"Sounds like a good idea. I'll see you in the morning, then, Callahan."

I saluted and left his office just as Todd was arriving. I stopped him before he went inside. "What happened? What did those bastards tell you?"

"Well, I imagine the same thing they told you. That we are suspected of being lovers and they intend to discharge us. They asked all sorts of questions about our relationship, to which I insisted that we were merely friends. They wouldn't tell me who said what about us to get this thing started, so I really wouldn't cooperate much with them. Oh, and they offered to set me up with the base shrink."

"Yeah, same bullshit as with me. Okay, you're gonna go in there and this asshole sergeant will give you a paper to sign acknowledging that the Air Force is moving to chuck you out. I refused to sign it before talking with a lawyer. Then he's gonna tell you to report to the disciplinary barracks as we are both relieved of duty. I've got it set up with Captain Blackman that we'll work in admin for him or someone else. I'm supposed to report at 0800 hours in the morning. He let me have the rest of the day off to get an attorney. After you see the sergeant, ask to see the captain. I'll wait for you over at the bench by the flag."

"Okay. See you there shortly. I just can't believe this shit."

As I walked toward the bench, my head began to spin. How was it possible to go from a hero with medals, to being processed out of the Air Force? Who ratted us out? I was determined to find out who the rat was but had no idea about how to go about it. As I sat there and stewed in my own juices, the squadron commander was driving by. He stopped when he saw me sitting on the bench. "Callahan, come over here," he ordered.

I got up and walked over to his car window and saluted. "Yes, sir?"

"You look like you lost your best friend, sitting there like that. Are you feeling all right, Callahan?"

"Not really, Major. In fact, I'm in a state of shock and frankly feel sick to my stomach over what's just happened to me and Sergeant Claymore."

"Happened? What's just happened to you and Claymore?"

"Well, sir, we were both called in by the OSI and told we are under investigation for being gay. We've denied it and we were ordered to report to Captain Blackman's office, where we were told by the clerk that the Air Force was moving to discharge us both. Claymore is at the captain's office as we speak."

"OSI, huh? Let me look into this, Callahan. Where have you been told to report for duty?"

"Well, at first, sir, we were told to report to the disciplinary barracks, but Captain Blackman told me to report for admin duty in his office starting in the morning. He wants to use my admin ability and I think he is going to do the same for Claymore."

"You go back to Captain Blackman, and tell him that I've ordered you to report to me in the morning for duty and that you are now my clerk until further notice. Tell the captain to put Claymore in his office for now."

"Thank you so much, major. You have no idea how much we appreciate this."

"For now, don't let this upset you too much. Let me take a look."

"Yes, sir." I saluted and the major drove away.

I headed back to Blackman's office to relay the orders of the squadron commander. Just as I got there, Todd was coming out of the captain's outer office.

"I just ran into the major and he ordered me to report to him in the morning and for you to report here. Is that the duty assignment the captain gave you?"

"Yeah, I'm to work on some backlog of some kind. He also said you would be working here."

"Okay, let me relay the new orders, and then we need to go home and start calling attorneys. I have an idea in that regard."

After passing on the orders from the major, I left the captain's office and we got in Todd's car and drove home. Neither one of us said much as we were deep in our own thoughts. This was not something we had even considered as a possibility since we lived off base and were careful on base. The first time we had slipped was in front of Sergeant Gray when he saw us kiss when the world was about to blow up. Could it have been the sergeant?

After getting settled back at the house, Todd cracked open a couple of beers and asked, "So, what's your idea?"

"Just listen," I replied as I picked up the phone. I dialed a number and waited for the party to answer. "Yes, is Judge Maxwell there, please?"

Todd frowned. "Yes. Would you tell him it's Airman Callahan from Warren calling?"

As I was on hold, Todd couldn't wait. "Why are you calling some judge?"

"Do you—" I began to ask Todd when I heard a voice on the other end of the line. "Ahh, yes, Judge Maxwell, how are you? Do you remember me?"

"Of course, airman, how are you? I haven't seen you since that first speeding ticket you brought before me just after you went on duty with the Warren base police."

"Yes, sir. That was the last time. Look, I know you're a busy man so I will get right to the reason for my call. My close friend and I are in trouble and we need a lawyer. I was hoping you might consider taking up our problem for us."

"In trouble with whom?"

"The Air Force, sir."

"Okay, give me a ten-second version of the issue."

"Well, Judge, I along with my roommate have been accused of being gay and the Air Force wants to chuck us out. Would you be uncomfortable representing us before the Air Force since you are a federal magistrate?"

"No, not at all. Look, we'd better meet as soon as possible. When are you available?"

"Have you had lunch yet, sir?"

"No. I was getting ready to go out in a few minutes. Do you want to meet for lunch somewhere?"

"Yes, Judge. How about the silver diner down on the corner of Missile Drive and Randolph Street?"

"Okay, the food is good there. Say in about twenty minutes?"

"Okay, Judge. Thank you and we will see you shortly."

I hung up and Todd just stared at me. "You know a federal magistrate?"

"Yes. Right after I got here, we started issuing civilian speeding tickets on base under the new federal law that mandated it. Well, I was the first base cop to issue a ticket to a civilian, a taxi cab driver, and the guy contested it. It went before a federal magistrate because he is the only one who has jurisdiction over the base where the ticket was issued. The city and state courts don't have jurisdiction to hear the case. So, that's how I know the judge. We talked for a while after I testified and the case was finalized with a finding of guilty."

"And why do you think this is the right guy to defend us?"

"Because, my dear, he *is* a federal magistrate, and an attorney, of course. He'll know the judge advocate general on base, and if we have him representing us, it can only be a good thing."

"All right. Let's get going; I don't want to be late for this guy."

"Give me your cell phone; I want to call Sergeant Gray at home while we're heading to the diner."

As Todd drove, I hesitated after another thought because I would be waking Gray up from sleeping. Since I really didn't have a choice, I called him anyway.

After several rings, a sleepy voice answered the phone. "Sergeant Gray."

"Sergeant Gray, first I apologize sincerely for waking you up, but this is most urgent."

"Callahan? Okay, what is it?"

"Sergeant, Claymore and I were hauled into the OSI office this morning and accused of being gay. We've been relieved of duty and the process to discharge us has been begun. We're en route right now to meet with the federal magistrate who I had that civvies speeding ticket in front of, to ask him to represent us with the Air Force. I don't trust Air Force attorneys right now."

"Oh, for fuck's sake! Don't those idiots have anything better to investigate but the sex lives of my men? A dozen damn Soviet commandos can get on base and kill our guys, but let there be a gay guy anywhere within a hundred miles of the base and those bastards are all over it."

"Sergeant, I have to ask you this, and I apologize in advance for asking it."

"Did I turn you two in? The answer is no."

"I had to ask, sergeant. I hope you understand. We're gonna tell the private attorney that it's all bullshit. I would be surprised if the OSI doesn't ask you if you know anything."

"Look, Bryce, I have never seen you two having sex, therefore I do not know if you are gay or not and that will continue to be my response to anyone's question, if asked. Now, may I go back to sleep?"

"Yes. Sorry again for waking you."

"Wait! Where are you two assigned? Not the barracks, I hope?"

"No, Sergeant. I've been assigned to be the major's clerk, and Claymore has been assigned to Captain Blackman to assist administratively with some backlog he has."

"You're shitting me! You guys get relieved of duty and then get put into two key spots within the command structure for the squadron? Unreal.... I need you both armed and on duty. Now I have to train another desk sergeant while you screw around with this crap. Okay. Get this thing taken care of and get back to duty as soon as you can."

The phone went dead. Todd glanced over and asked, "Was he mad? I could hear him all the way over here like he was in the backseat!"

"Yeah, but not at us. With the system. He wants us back as soon as possible, and will not divulge what he has seen and knows. We stick with the strategy that we are not gay. Otherwise, we give up our Air Force careers and any future career in law enforcement."

As we walked into the diner, I looked around at the tables and booths, trying to recognize the judge off the bench and out of his robe.

Finally, I spotted him in a booth way in the back and we headed over and took the seat opposite from him.

"Airman, good to see you again," he said.

"Likewise. This is Sergeant Todd Claymore, the other party to this mess."

They shook hands and then he got down to business as soon as the waitress took our lunch orders.

"First of all, I will represent you both before the Air Force. In fact, I know Colonel O'Dell, who is the judge advocate general on base. In case you don't know it, he has the final say-so on the legal strength of the Air Force's case and can send this to a court-martial or dismiss the case with a wave of his hand. After we finish here today, I will make an appointment to see him. Do you have Air Force counsel?"

"No, sir. After all this going on, I don't trust anyone in that office."

"Well, I'm gonna need to have a liaison that is committed to our side in this case. Many things I can do through him and save myself the time of doing it myself. For this reason, I'm only going to charge you guys a hundred dollars to handle this case. That does two things: it acts as a legal retainer for me, and it covers minor expenses that will come up. Now, if for some reason we go to court-martial, and I defend you both, then we have to talk some serious money, as that takes a lot of time and preparation. Fortunately, my magistrate duties are usually light. As you'll recall, you were the only case that day in my courtroom, Bryce."

"Yes, sir, I remember. A hundred bucks is more than generous of you, Judge, and I appreciate it as does Todd."

"Look, guys, let's talk turkey here. Now, I'm no bigot, and I don't hate gay people. Having said that, I need total honesty out of you both to the following questions. Regardless of your answers, I'm gonna represent you both and try to keep you in the Air Force if that's what you want."

Todd and I looked at each other and nodded. "Okay, shoot," I said.

"Do they have any evidence that you two are gay?"

"We don't know. They won't tell us what they have or even what we are accused of, or who alleged what," I replied.

"Okay, that tells me they are weak right off. The next question is, what is there lying around that they might find to implicate you?"

"If you mean gay magazines, movies, stuff like that—nothing. They could find nothing because there is nothing to find," Todd answered.

"Are either or both of you gay?"

Just then the waitress put down our orders and walked away. While she was there, I took out my checkbook and wrote out a check for $100 and slid it across the table to the judge. He was now officially retained. He took the check without looking at it and folded it and put it into his jacket. He smiled at me in a knowing way.

"Yes, you have now conveyed your retainer to me, which officially makes me your lawyer."

"The answer to your question is yes. We are both gay. We are lovers. We don't know how anyone else knows it or what they might have whispered into the ear of OSI."

"You're sure you both have been very discreet? You've not gone to any gay bars in town or any other place gays hang out?"

"Well, Cheyenne has only one tiny gay bar and it is a dump. So, the answer is no," Todd answered.

"There is one person who knows for sure that we are gay, and that's our flight sergeant, Sergeant Gray. While Todd was recuperating from a gunshot wound received from the Russian commandos, he was at the desk one night recently when the world was about to end. We really did think we were done, and we exchanged a quick kiss and Sergeant Gray walked in and saw us. He was not upset and told us he didn't care as long as we did our jobs."

"You were wounded recently?"

"Yes, I'm just about healed up now."

"Judge, we received a few medals a couple of days ago, and I even received a Bronze Star and a Silver Star for bravery."

"And now they're trying to kick you out because you're gay. Incredible. How do you know it wasn't this Sergeant Gray who turned you guys in?"

"Well, for one we know him fairly well, and he is a fair man. We believed him when he said it didn't matter to him that we were gay. Plus, I called him on the way here and asked him if he had turned us in and he said no. I believe him."

"I've got to try and get a look at what they have. What else did they say or do?"

"They wanted me to allow them to search our off-base housing immediately. When I said I wanted to consult an attorney first, they said in that case, they would withdraw the request."

"Well, obviously they hoped to have you say yes, search your house, and find incriminating evidence of your relationship, to strengthen their case against you both. They weren't interested after you advised them about an attorney because you would then have a chance to clean anything like that up and the search would be worthless. I'm glad you denied their request. Now, you are both represented by counsel. Any questioning of either of you by the OSI or anyone else related to this investigation must not be done without me being present. In an emergency, your Air Force lawyer will have to do. I suggest you obtain one and let me know his name this afternoon. Also advise him that you have retained my services and give him my number. Don't be insubordinate or hostile with anyone from the Air Force. Do not give them an alternate route to dismissing you because they can't get you on the gay charge. Now, if you have no questions, I must run. I have a lot of work to do preparing for this."

Todd asked, "Judge, should we tell the Air Force attorney that we're gay if he asks?"

"Yes. No sense in lying to them. They can't betray your confidence or they would be disbarred same as if they were civilians."

"What's the next step? Will you contact Todd or me about interviews or will we be calling you?"

"The Air Force is not required to tell me first that they are going to interview you, but they can't proceed to do so without me. Chances are they'll leave it up to you to tell me."

"Okay, one final question: What's your gut reaction on this matter? Do we have a chance of beating this thing?"

"Well, without knowing exactly what information they have, I can't be sure. But I will say this: You are both combat medal winners of recent vintage, with one of you earning a Purple Heart, and the other a Bronze and Silver Star. If all they have is an allegation, they don't stand a chance. If, however, they have someone like Sergeant Gray who has seen something, then they've got a shot. We may have to take this to a court-martial. I just don't know yet."

"Okay, thank you, Judge. I guess we'll be talking soon."

With that the judge got up and left the diner. Todd and I sat at the table in a deep mood of depression. "Let's get out of here," I said.

When we got back to our house, we both just collapsed on the sofa. I was overcome with emotion that had built up over the missile crisis and now this on top of it. Tears flooded my eyes and when Todd saw the shape I was in, he took me in his arms and held me tight.

"Don't worry; we're both strong and we're gonna fight this shit. I can't believe they are actually going to try and throw us out after having just won medals defending this country."

"That's what you don't understand though, Todd. It doesn't matter to these assholes what we've done for the Air Force. They're on a witch hunt, and they won't stop until they are burning a witch at the stake. I mean, who needs this shit? Maybe we should just tell them to shove the Air Force and get out and start our life. What's wrong with that?"

"That would let the bastards win then, wouldn't it? You want them smiling as we walk out the front gate? You want them to put two more notches on their gun belt? Fuck 'em. We'll fight, and what's more, we'll win."

After a couple more minutes, I was able to gather myself together, and I called the base legal office. I told the airman who answered the phone that we needed an attorney. An appointment was set up for the next morning at 1000 hours.

That night as we lay in bed holding each other, I became emotional again. Todd didn't say anything this time; he just held me. I knew things would work out, but the stress was finally just too much for me. My pride was now on the line along with everything else. I was determined that the Air Force wouldn't take that.

CHAPTER 12

THE next morning, I reported for duty at the squadron commander's office and Todd reported in at the captain's office. As I went by the base police desk area, the other guys looked at me funny and no one said a thing. This wasn't my shift on duty so I wasn't as familiar with these guys as I was with my own flight friends. Nevertheless, word was getting around quickly about what was happening.

The clerk who was the comedian wasn't around and so I just took my place at his desk and began to answer the phone and take messages. After a few minutes, the major came down from upstairs and walked up to the desk as I was hanging up the phone.

"Good morning, Callahan. How are you doing?"

"Good morning, sir. I'm hanging in. You would think I had something catchable by the way the guys out there just stared at me on my way in this morning. I guess word is spreading."

"Of course it is. Nothing juicer than a sex scandal, Callahan. You should know that. My usual clerk is on thirty-day leave, so you will handle all his normal duties. I'll have some letters that need to be typed up later."

"Yes, sir, but I have to tell you that I have an appointment at base legal at 1000 hours. Will that be a problem, sir?"

"No. Just let me know when you are going."

"Yes, sir."

I wanted to make the major happy that he chose me to take the duty station I had been assigned to rather than wasting away in the disciplinary barracks. I typed up all the letters he needed done before I went to the appointment with base legal. When it was time to go, I walked into his office and advised him I was leaving for my appointment and put a file folder into his in-basket before I left. Once again, as I walked by my former duty station, I got a glaring look from the current on-duty desk sergeant. *Fuck 'em,* I thought, and managed to smile to myself.

Todd was already waiting for me when I got there and I smiled when I saw him. He smiled back but looked worried.

"They said when you got here to go into the conference room and they would be right in," he said.

"Okay, let's get this circus started."

Just after taking our seats, two Air Force lawyers walked in and sat down.

"Okay, I'm Captain McKlosky, and this is Captain Brookhall. We have been assigned to your case as defense counsel. Now, we understand that you have hired a local attorney, is that right?"

"Yes, we hired Judge Maxwell as lead defense counsel on this case. He requested that we secure Air Force representation as well, with him being lead counsel."

"Why did you feel that it was necessary to hire a civilian, Airman Callahan?"

"We would just feel better having a civilian attorney who is familiar with the federal court system involved in this case. Frankly, I don't trust the Air Force one bit, and feel better having an attorney who won't hesitate to go into court if we need to."

"Well, just so you know, we are bound by the same level of confidentiality that a civilian attorney would be. So, anything you tell us, we can't reveal without your permission. So, let's get started. You both are accused of being gay. Are you?"

I looked at Todd and then back to the attorneys. "Yes. We are a couple. We don't hang out in bars, we don't do anything to draw attention to ourselves, and we are very discreet. We have been unable to determine what the OSI has on us. Do you know?" I asked.

"No, we don't. The way this works is that we first interview you, see the charge, which we have, and then the case begins to unfold. OSI will eventually have to give us everything, but right now they are in the investigative phase and do not have to reveal anything other than the allegation for the time being. It may well be another four weeks before we see the details."

"Well, that's just great. So in the meantime we have to sit around in a state of anxiety, suspended from our duties, facing the possibility of discharge, and put up with the dirty looks and whispers. Fuck." Todd was not pleased.

"I know it's going to be rough on both of you, but there is no alternative unless you just want to admit that you are gay and let the Air Force discharge you. That would take about a week altogether."

"That is not an option," I replied.

"No way," Todd added.

"Very well, then. That's all for now. We will talk with Judge Maxwell and coordinate the next steps. In the meantime, stay out of trouble. Where are you two working—the discharge barracks?"

"No, sir. I'm my squadron commander's clerk, and Todd is the squadron administrative officer's clerk."

"You two are up for discharge, and yet your commander puts you both in sensitive positions of that caliber? Well, that's the first time that has happened in all the time I've been here and handled these types of cases. There is no doubt in my mind that you both enjoy the respect of your commanding officers. This is a good thing."

"So, there have been other proceedings to discharge gay airmen?"

"Dozens. This is fairly routine."

"Maybe for you and the Air Force. Okay. We'll stay in touch," I said.

AS we both walked back toward our respective offices, Todd began to let his anger out.

"I just can't fucking believe all this shit. We both love the Air Force, we both love our jobs, and we love each other. Everything was going along incredibly well, including having survived a firefight with Soviet commandos. Now, we're witches being hunted in sixteenth-century Salem, Massachusetts, by a pair of grinning idiots who think we're stupid. Life just fucking sucks, Bryce!"

"Yeah, none of this is fair, but no one ever told us life was supposed to be fair. Okay. Worst-case scenario: They discharge us for being gay. We choose a city to start the rest of our lives together and go for it. Maybe I'm being naive, but I believe that as long as we have each other, we can overcome any obstacle in our way to happiness. We would also not have to worry about whether or not we can pull off our next duty assignment to the same base in Europe."

I left Todd at his building and continued on back to the base police headquarters building. The major was in a meeting, so I just went back to sorting the incoming mail. As I opened various envelopes and sorted which letter went where, I found a large envelope marked to the attention of the commanding officer of the 91st Security Police Squadron, eyes only. The return address on the envelope stated, "OSI, F.E. Warren Air Force Base, Cheyenne, Wyoming."

If the envelope had been facedown, I would have just opened it up and not even realized who it was from. Should I open the envelope? I almost broke out in a cold sweat trying to decide what to do. The phone rang, interrupting my decision, and I took care of the caller's problem and then returned to my own.

I decided to open the envelope and see what there was to see. Inside was a file folder marked, "Confidential, eyes only." This meant that only the major was supposed to see inside the folder. As he was still in a meeting and no one was around, I took a peak. My blood ran cold as I read: "Investigative file on Airman Bryce Callahan and Sergeant Todd Claymore."

I had no intention of sitting there and reading the entire folder but I just had to find out who said what to start all of this. I quickly scanned down the report until I came to the part labeled "Allegation."

"This office was notified by a CI (confidential informant) that Callahan and Claymore were homosexually involved with each other and were carrying on a relationship in their off-base housing quarters. The CI reports that upon visiting the two at their home, he was about to knock on the door when he heard both airmen talking about being in love with each other and what Sergeant Claymore planned on doing to Airman Callahan that night in bed. The window to the right of the door was open and the CI was able to clearly hear the conversation. CI turned around and left the area without making his presence known. Additionally, CI is a security policeman assigned to the missile fields with the targets of this investigation and reports that both airmen were assigned to sleep in a camper vehicle on site during the recent special security procedures in the field. CI reports taking a walk late at night before he went to bed and after having approached the camper, reported to this office that he heard sounds of "love-making" coming from inside the camper. CI left the immediate area of the camper and returned to his own bunk."

I put the folder back into the envelope it came in and put it back on the desk. Just as I did that, the door to the major's office opened, and a couple of officers left as the meeting had ended. I took this opportunity to dispose of the opened envelope.

"Sir, this just came in the mail. I opened the envelope and then realized it's marked your eyes only." I gave the envelope to the major, who took it and put it on his desk and came back out to my desk.

"Callahan, you get that legal stuff taken care of?"

"Yes, sir. Sergeant Claymore and I now have Air Force counsel in addition to Judge Maxell, who we retained to represent us."

"Maxwell the local federal magistrate?"

"Yes, sir. He agreed to represent us in this matter."

"Okay. That was probably a good move. You'll find in my out-basket a couple of letters that need to be typed up, and the AWOL report is due out this afternoon. So, if you could take care of those two things before lunch, that would be great."

"Will do, sir."

THINGS ran pretty smoothly over the next couple of weeks and our anxiety levels began to drop somewhat. Todd was happy with his duties working for Captain Blackwell, and I was more than happy working for the major. The great mystery for us was trying to figure out who the rat was that had ran to the OSI and told tales. We narrowed it down to a couple of guys and we figured out one way to determine who it was.

We decided to have a little party and invited four guys from our old flight to come and have dinner and beer while we watched a football game that everyone was anticipating. We put the word out to the guys and waited to see what their reactions would be. Would they come?

Unfortunately, the ploy did not work. None of the guys accepted the invitation for fear of being suspected of being gay just for hanging out with us. I was disappointed that a simple approach to the problem didn't work. We decided we would more than likely not find out who it was unless we had to face a court-martial. Then the Air Force had to present our accuser to us in court. But fate intervenes in the end....

About a week later, another envelope came in from the OSI, and once again, I opened it. This time the report dealt with Airman Clyde Barksdale, who was a member of one of the security teams who were on site while we were in the field, but not directly on our team.

The report was to notify the major that Barksdale had been arrested by the Cheyenne Police for "indecent exposure" to an eighty-four-year-old woman. OSI conducted a preliminary investigation and confirmed the report of the incident with the elderly woman, who stated that Barksdale approached her in her own backyard at her house and dropped his trousers. She screamed and Barksdale ran. The Cheyenne Police picked him up within seven minutes of getting the call. He was positively identified by the victim.

The report went on to say that Barksdale's arrest could complicate another OSI investigation as he was the CI on a 39-12 discharge case that was in progress. A 39-12 discharge was a discharge for being gay. It was this son of a bitch who had ratted out Todd and me. This self-righteous jerk, who just had to out us to OSI, was himself a pervert who exposed himself in public to little old ladies. Usually with those guys, their conduct was ongoing when they were arrested for the first time. There could be countless victims in the Cheyenne area.

I smiled to myself and put away the file. This would be a serious blow to the Air Force's case against Todd and me. In fact, I didn't know how they could proceed with the case if he was their only witness to anything. This time, I simply placed the envelope, resealed, into the major's inbox. If I was questioned about it, I would simply say that I had once again just opened the envelope without paying attention to who it was from. I couldn't wait to tell Todd.

I picked up the phone and dialed his office.

"Captain Blackman's office, Sergeant Claymore speaking. May I help you, sir?"

"Todd, Bryce. Can you talk?"

"Yeah, what's up?"

"You can relax a bit. The Air Force just stubbed its toe on our case and it will almost surely guarantee that the case will be dropped."

"How? What happened? Are you sure? Tell me!"

Before I could answer, the major returned, walking down the hallway toward his office and my desk. "Well, that's all I have for now. We'll be sure to notify you if anything changes. Thank you."

I hung up. "Good afternoon, sir."

"Callahan. You look happy for a change; any particular reason?"

"No, sir. Just enjoying my job working for you, sir."

"Callahan, you're not a kiss-ass, so you're up to something. I better keep an eye on you," he said, walking into his office and chuckling.

I quickly finished up the letters that had to be typed and took them into the major's office. As I turned around to leave, he stopped me.

"Callahan, I see you opened another OSI envelope. Another accident?"

"Ah, yes, sir. Sorry, sir. I resealed the envelope once I realized where it came from, sir."

The major smiled as he leaned back in his chair. "You didn't happen to read the contents of the file, did you?"

"No, sir. I can honestly say I did not read the contents of that file, sir." After all, I hadn't read the contents, only two paragraphs.

"Okay, good. 'Cause if you had read the contents, you might be in a good mood and smiling inexplicably."

"Oh. Maybe so, sir."

"You might also be planning on resuming your desk duties soon as well."

"Oh? That good, sir? That must be quite the envelope, sir."

"Well, Callahan, I certainly can't discuss the contents of OSI reports with my clerk, but suffice it to say, I might miss you terribly were you to resume your old duties. You've been a fantastic clerk and you'll be hard to replace, Bryce."

"Thank you, sir. I'm sure Sergeant Claymore will miss his working for the captain as well, sir."

"Yes, that is true. Carry on, Callahan."

I smiled and said, "Yes, sir."

THAT night Todd and I celebrated the only way we knew how to celebrate this type of good news. First, we closed all the windows in the house. Second, we pulled all the curtains and blinds so that no one could see into the house. And finally, we made love all night long and fell asleep two hours before the sun came up.

That next afternoon, we had a meeting at the judge advocate general's office on base. Present would be all three of our lawyers, the JAG, and an OSI agent. The purpose of the meeting was to dispose of the discharge proceedings or initiate a court-martial. We dressed in Class A dress blues, and reported as ordered at 1400 hours.

When the JAG entered the conference room, we stood up and were told to be seated. Judge Maxell opened the meeting.

"Colonel, it's time we requested a look at the file on my clients' behalf. We still do not know what the accusations are and who is making them. Without this information, we cannot prepare for any future proceedings."

"Very well, Judge. Here's the file."

We sat there in silence while Judge Maxwell and our two Air Force attorneys went over the contents of the Air Force's case against us. After about five minutes, the judge looked up.

"Thank you, Colonel. Do I take it that the only thing that the discharge is proposed upon is the word of one airman who alleges to hearing things and nothing else?"

"That is correct, Judge."

"The OSI was unable to find any evidence of a homosexual relationship between my clients?"

"That is correct, Judge. I have to tell you that I have never seen another case as weak as this one."

"Judge, we demand a court-martial."

"I don't blame you one bit! I would also if I were in your shoes. Agent Martinez, does your office have any other evidence or information to indicate that these men are what you allege?"

"No, sir, but given time, we feel confident that we can develop more evidence and even use the polygraph."

"You mean make up evidence!" I said before I could shut my mouth.

The judge put his hand on my arm to restrain any further thinking out loud.

"Sorry, Colonel. This whole thing has been stressful."

"Understood, airman. So, Agent Martinez, your entire case rests on the word of a man who has, since making these accusations, been himself arrested for a sex-related offense. Is that correct?"

"Yes, sir, I'm afraid it is."

The colonel took back the case file from the judge and wrote on the inside cover of the file. "Gentlemen, this matter is dismissed. I cannot bring this matter forward based on such trivial nonsense as the OSI has presented in this matter. This doesn't even begin to mention the fact that both of the accused were recently awarded honors and medals by the Air Force for bravery in action against the enemy! It seems to me that the OSI would be better utilized by investigating things other than the alleged sex lives of the men of this command. Sergeant Claymore and Airman Callahan, you are both restored to full duty with all attending clearances, responsibilities, and privileges. Report to your commanding officer for further orders. My office will contact the major's office forthwith."

"Thank you, Colonel," I said.

"Good to see you again, Judge. You really must come out to the officers' club once in a while; it's been too long."

Our lawyers shook hands with Todd and me, and we left the meeting on cloud nine. We ducked into the restroom before leaving the building and, once we were sure no one was in there, we hugged each other and laughed quietly. We felt positively giddy.

We left the JAG building and headed first to Captain Blackwell's office where we found him in his usual place behind his desk. After telling him about what happened, he got up and shook both our hands and said, "I'm relieved. The Air Force cannot afford to lose men of your caliber. Sergeant, do you think you could finish out the week here with helping me catch up on the backlog of work?"

"Yes, sir, if you'll square it away with the major."

"Okay, I'll take care of that. Why don't you take off for an hour and then report back for duty?"

"Yes, sir. Will do," Todd responded.

"I just wanted to thank you one more time, Captain, for your compassion and caring in assigning us to work that allowed us to maintain our dignity. We won't forget it."

"Don't give it another thought. I knew you men would be cleared. Now you both better report to the major."

AFTER reporting back to the major as ordered by the JAG, the major congratulated us on clearing our names. "Callahan, I knew the contents of that last report that you didn't read would be the end of that crap. You men ready to get back to your real jobs?"

"Well, sir, the captain asked if I could stay the remainder of the week to finish helping him get caught up and I have no objection if you clear it, sir."

"Yes, no problem with that. In fact, Callahan, you stay put through the end of the week as well, and both of you report for duty with Sergeant Gray on Monday. In the meantime, be sure to pick up your weapons cards from the armory. I'll let them know you're restored to duty."

We thanked the major one more time, saluted, and left the office. It would be good to go home at the end of this day.

CHAPTER 13

MORE than a month had passed since Todd and I had been restored to duty and our lives were beginning to return to normal. Todd's shoulder was fully healed and our love life was back on track and creating havoc on the bedsprings. The only problem that continued was dirty looks from some of the men.

Even though we beat the system, the cloud of suspicion had been cast over us. In talking to Sergeant Gray about the situation, he agreed that nothing we could do short of getting married, to women, would ever make the rumors and innuendos go away. The simple fact of our having been suspended for being gay was enough for some in the ranks to forever hold a grudge against us and present a hostile attitude toward Todd and me. This began to kill our love for the Air Force, as it was impossible to ever get back to the way things were before we had been suspended.

Barksdale had blabbed all over the place about the information he had given to the OSI. This was enough to convict us in the eyes of some men. My only comfort with Barksdale was that the Air Force was far rougher on him than they ever were on Todd and me.

Barksdale was court-martialed and given a bad-conduct discharge as a result of his arrest and conviction on indecent exposure charges. He was tossed out of the Air Force. This fact didn't seem to convince any of his former friends that we were deserving of acceptance by our co-workers. Finally, one night I decided to talk to Todd about it.

"Look, honey, I'm having great difficulty in dealing with the whispers and all from some of the guys. Remember, our lives could depend on these same men. Can we trust them? I don't know. Here's what I'm thinking. Let me approach the major and ask that you and I be transferred to say, oh, I don't know, Italy maybe? I can just lay it out on the line with the major and tell him we think the Air Force owes us something for putting us through all that nonsense and that our reputations are ruined here at Warren. What do you think?"

"Wow. That's one way to deal with the issue. Do you think he'll go for it?"

"Why not? We are both decorated airmen now who have been fucked by the Air Force. A transfer isn't that unusual of a request under the circumstances and he really has no reason to say no. It also doesn't hurt that he likes both of us. I think he'll do it. Can I try?"

"Yeah, okay, but I want to be there also. After all, you're trying to get us both transferred and I want to make damn sure that we go to the same base. We can ask for Italy and see what he says."

"Okay. Let's talk to him tomorrow, then."

WE were on our two-day break, so we didn't have to worry about being able to catch him while we were on duty. A little after 0900 hours, we knocked on his office door. He still hadn't replaced me yet.

"Come in."

We walked in, saluted, and stood at attention. "Sir, do you have a moment to hear a request from us?"

"Of course. What's on your minds?"

I went into a detailed explanation of why we were requesting a transfer and to where. He understood what it was like for us, as he had been quietly monitoring the situation. In the end, he said he would do what he could to grant our request and told us he would let us know as soon as possible. As we turned to go after saluting, he stopped me.

"Callahan, since you're here, can I ask you to do something?"

"Of course, sir. What is it?"

"Can you type up these damn letters that have to go up to the general? I still don't have a decent clerk who can type without using his feet."

"Of course, sir. I'll have them all done within an hour."

Todd said he would go over to the chow hall for coffee and then come back to get me so we could go back home. I typed up the major's letters, chatted with him for a few more minutes, and then Todd came in and got me and we left.

LIFE went on as normal for another two weeks, until one morning while I was working the desk, the major came in.

"Callahan, your request for a transfer to Italy has been approved for both you and Claymore. You leave in two weeks. Report to the first sergeant's office and begin the process of clearing base. I take it you guys will want to take leave before going overseas, so you are relieved of your base duties at the end of your shift. Let Claymore know, and congratulations to you both. I will miss you. You've been a good man and a credit to the Air Force. Frankly, Callahan, I really don't care if you and Claymore are gay or not. You did your jobs, caused no problems outside of shooting snakes, and showed outstanding bravery in combat. I couldn't ask anything more of either one of you. You both have been a credit to this squadron and to the Air Force. I will be drawing up a letter to your new commanding officer in Italy. You'll have to type the damn thing, though. I will send it ahead of your arrival. I want him to know what kind of men he is getting."

The major then shook my hand, smiled, and left the desk. When Sergeant Gray came in off patrol, I informed him of the transfer. He was upset at losing us right after having just gotten us back from the suspension. Nonetheless, he was very happy for us and told us we would love Italy.

The end of the shift came, and I signed off on my last desk sergeant's report at Francis E. Warren Air Force Base. Next stop: Italy, and the beginning of the rest of our lives together.

Try these other titles from John….

JOHN SIMPSON, a Vietnam era Veteran, has been a uniformed Police Officer of the year, a Federal Agent, a Federal Magistrate, an armed bodyguard to royalty and a senior Government executive, with awards from the Vice-President of the United States and the Secretary of the Treasury. John now writes and is the author of "Condor One" and "Murder Most Gay," with a sequel entitled "Task Force," all available through Dreamspinner Press, and numerous short stories for Alyson Books. Additionally, he has written articles for various gay and straight magazines. John has legally married his long time companion and lives with Jack, who he has been with for almost 35 years, and their three wonderful Scott Terriers, all spoiled and a breed of canine family member that is unique in dogdom. John is also involved with the Old Catholic Church and its liberal pastoral positions on the Gay community.

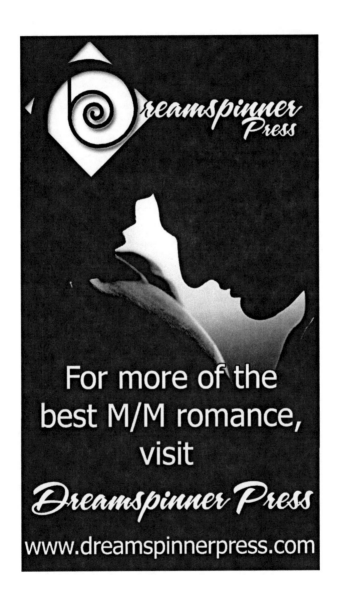

Printed in the United States
145018LV00004B/28/P

9 781935 192596